BRAD WILLIAMS

THE DEAD KING'S BONES

For my wife and soul mate

Denise

Thank you for providing me with the motivation to start writing and get my stories published!

Contents

Prologue

It had been two long years since the fall of Kanarzand and the corruption that smothered the Tahnaar Desert. The once-proud frontier town, once a hub of discovery, magic, and ambition, lay in ruins after the defeat of The Twelve and the rise of the dark entity Izen'draazt. His dark minions had swept across the desert like a plague, twisting the sands with corruption and choking the life from the land. Darkness reigned, and for a time, hope seemed distant.

But the rogue mercenaries, led by the former Argar farmer named Thaxos, who had once sought to hunt down Aidan to the ends of the world made a decision that changed the course of history. United by their vow of vengeance, they stormed the dark temple of Izen'draazt, confronting the ancient evil in its lair. It was not an easy battle. Some of them fell to the dark magic, the crushing weight of an evil force that had been growing for millennia. But in the end, they prevailed. Izen'draazt was defeated, his physical form destroyed, and his dark influence shattered.

Gideon City had survived and with it, New Kanarzand had grown and thrived on its fringes, still under the control of The Arcane Council and the stern and omnipresent over watch of The High Magocracy.

The moment the rogue mercenaries drove the final blow into Izen'draazt, the desert itself seemed to breathe again. The sky, once blood-red and filled with swirling black clouds, cleared. The air, heavy with malice, lightened. Slowly, the corrupted sands began to regenerate, under the direction of the Wasteland Druid and his new Destari followers, allowing life to return to the desert that had once been a barren wilderness. What had seemed like an inevitable descent into chaos was reversed, and now, a new chapter for the Tahnaar Desert was beginning.

1

Aidan's Dreams

Aidan awoke with a violent start, his entire body drenched in sweat, heart pounding so fiercely he feared it might burst.

He clutched his chest, fingers digging into his flesh as he tried to quell the burning sensation that radiated through his shoulder and chest. The pain, searing and all-encompassing, lingered just long enough to leave him disoriented and gasping.

His room aboard the Zephyr Breeze was dark, quiet except for the soft creaks of the airship as it cut through the night sky on its journey toward Kharadia, homeland of the Aystar people. Yet, as familiar as his surroundings were, Aidan could not shake the remnants of the dream; the latest in a string of nightmares that seemed determined to carve away at his very soul.

In each of these dreams, there was something watching him, something unseen but undeniably close, lurking in the shadows just beyond his sight. Its presence filled him with a suffocating dread, a visceral fear that clawed its way into his chest and left him breathless. Yet, against every instinct to flee, there was an inexplicable pull, a terrible compulsion that urged him to let it come closer, to surrender to its influence, to... trust it. The duality of terror and attraction left him shaken, like a moth caught between the seductive glow of the flame and the inevitable death it promised.

And then there was the storm. Dark, ominous clouds would roll across the skies, lightning flaring within their depths and casting jagged, monstrous shadows that crawled across the land beneath his feet. He felt the storm in his bones; it hummed and buzzed with an electric energy that made his skin prickle, and his breath quicken. He stood alone in that dreamscape, watching as the tempest gathered strength, whipping the world around him into a chaotic, thrashing frenzy.

But it was the burning that always broke him. Every time, without fail, as the storm grew more intense, he would feel a flame ignite somewhere deep inside him. It would begin as a dull heat in his chest, then quickly swell until it became unbearable, radiating outward from one singular, unidentifiable point. It was as if something was trying to escape him, something that had been buried within, fighting to break free and consume him from the inside out. And every time, just as the heat threatened to overwhelm him, Aidan would awaken, gasping and clutching at his chest, his mind a whirlwind of confusion and dread.

Lying back now, Aidan closed his eyes and tried to slow his breathing, counting each exhale until the rapid thumping of his heart began to subside. The Zephyr Breeze's gentle movements reassured him, but only barely. These dreams, which he had first dismissed as simple nightmares, were becoming more intense, more vivid, and, disturbingly, more painful. There was no denying it: something in him was changing, and whatever was happening in these dreams felt far too real to ignore.

He knew he needed to tell someone, that keeping such vivid visions a secret might only serve to make them worse. But even as he considered the idea, a visceral resistance welled up within him. The thought of sharing these dreams with Ahlissa or Jillian - or anyone on the Zephyr Breeze, for that matter - felt like a betrayal of some kind. There was a part of him that felt as though these visions were meant for him alone, as though he were bearing witness to something ancient, something that others might neither understand nor accept. How could he possibly explain the compulsion he felt, the desire to draw closer to that lurking, ominous force?

This was not simply a matter of sharing his fear; it was as though admitting to these dreams would somehow unleash them into the waking world, drawing that malevolent presence out of his mind and into the light. He shuddered at the thought, forcing himself to sit up and stretch his arms, as if motion might help dispel the weight of dread pressing down on him.

He rose from his bed and paced across the small cabin, each step calculated, controlled. Even in the dim light, his surroundings were comforting: the neatly stacked books he had brought aboard, the scabbard containing his enchanted longsword leaning against the wall, his personal journal resting on the table, where he had scribbled hurried notes about Aethyr Marks and a name from his dreams ... Kale Ashtari. Here, in this modest cabin, he should have felt safe, removed from the forces of darkness that roamed in his dreams.

But tonight, the very air felt charged, as though remnants of the storm had slipped through the boundaries of sleep and reality. His skin prickled, and his chest tightened once again, not from pain this time but from a gnawing anticipation, a feeling that something was watching him, even now. He found himself drawn to the small porthole, looking out over the vast, empty night sky. Stars dotted the expanse, twinkling serenely, oblivious to his inner turmoil.

Aidan's fingers instinctively brushed over the fabric of his shirt where the burning sensation had originated. He knew, somehow, that this was more than just an effect of his taint or some lingering connection to the Aethyr Mark that had marked him long ago. There was something deeper at play here, something ancient, something that had been awakened within him. His thoughts turned to his bloodline, and to the reference of Kale Ashtari; the name felt strangely familiar, and he considered it might be connected. The symbol he had seen in his dreams, the one that seemed burned into his chest with every nightmare, bore a striking resemblance to the marks he had read about in the old scrolls.

But those marks were supposed to be remnants of a bygone age, traces of power that had vanished with the fall of the Kale Ashtari. They weren't meant to resurface, not like this, not burning and clawing their way into the present. If he told anyone about these dreams, would they believe him? And if they did, would they see him as something dangerous, someone to be feared?

Aidan knew his private studies were revealing ancient secrets, some might call it dark knowledge, to him. His research into it was becoming obsessive and he knew some academic institutions and even the High Magocracy in Gideon City would frown upon his work if they knew the full extent that he had truly discovered.

With a deep sigh, Aidan returned to his bed, but he didn't lie down.

Instead, he sat on the edge, head in his hands, wrestling with the weight of his secrets. He had always been wary of the power he held within himself, careful not to draw too much attention to the strange abilities his taint sometimes granted him. But now, with these dreams - these visions - he knew he was treading a thin line between control and surrender. If he gave in to that compulsion, if he allowed himself to draw closer to whatever it was that beckoned him, he might uncover the truth of his heritage. But at what cost?

The idea of revealing these dreams to Ahlissa or Jillian seemed increasingly dangerous. He couldn't risk letting them see him as a threat. And deep down, he feared that if he spoke these visions aloud, he might somehow make them more real, binding himself to the dark entity that lurked within them. He would carry this burden alone, for as long as he could bear it, and hope that the dreams would not consume him in the process.

Aidan finally lay back down, staring up at the ceiling as he willed himself to calm. But sleep would not come easily. Every time he closed his eyes, he saw flashes of the storm, heard the low, rumbling laughter of something that awaited him in the shadows. And though he tried to shake the feeling, he knew that this was only the beginning. Whatever was calling to him in those dreams was growing stronger, and soon, he would have to face it - alone.

He would need to be vigilant, maintaining the facade of control while carrying the weight of the nightmares in silence. His chest still tingled with the memory of that searing pain, and he could almost feel the eyes of the unseen watcher upon him. The feeling was a constant reminder that he was not as alone as he might wish to be, that something else moved in the darkness, shadowing his every step. And as the Zephyr

Breeze continued its journey, soaring over the vast, uncharted expanse, Aidan knew that his path was set.

He lay awake, heart pounding, awaiting the night's end, knowing that he would meet the darkness again soon, and that each time, it drew a little closer.

2

The Ceremony of Mourning and Celebration

As the Zephyr Breeze neared Sunhold, capital city of the Aystar in Kharadia, Aidan gazed out from the ship's deck, entranced by the cityscape unfolding before him. Sunhold rose majestically on a mountainous plateau, nestled within a stunning range of peaks that shimmered in the dawn light. The city was a marvel, an intricate fusion of architectural grace and ancient grandeur that radiated power and wisdom. Aidan felt a mixture of awe and anticipation; this was the fabled homeland of the Aystar and Khystar people, a place where his own long-buried heritage intertwined with the city's legendary past.

From the distance, the golden rooftops of Sunhold's grand temples and palaces glittered like beacons. The city sprawled over terraced levels, each layer of Sunhold seemingly more glorious than the last. The structures were a blend of marble and gold-veined stone, their facades adorned with intricate carvings of winged figures, mythical beasts, and scenes from the ancient histories of the Aystar. Ornate domes rose from temples dedicated to various ancestral deities, some capped with golden spires that reached high into the sky, reflecting the sunlight in all directions. The effect was blindingly radiant, almost as if the city itself was channelling celestial light.

Closer to the heart of Sunhold stood the Library of Ancients, an enormous multi-tiered building that seemed to command the very landscape. Its walls were crafted from polished stone that shimmered with a pearlescent quality. The Library towered over the other buildings, a testament to the Aystaran peoples' reverence for knowledge. Legends claimed it held scrolls and tomes dating back to the Age of Calamity, documenting the histories and secrets of the Aystar and Khystar. For Aidan, it was as if his dreams had come to life; an entire city built to preserve the wisdom and mysteries of his people, both known and hidden.

As the Zephyr Breeze approached the docking platforms that extended from Sunhold's lower levels, Aidan marvelled at the craftsmanship of the structures. The platforms were supported by wide marble columns inlaid with bands of shining silver metal, decorated with patterns that glowed faintly with Aethyr-infused magic. Thin streams of light, a mix of magical and natural energy, cascaded down the sides of the city's terraces, giving the appearance of golden rivers running from one level to the next. The sound of these luminous cascades mingled with the soft hum of magical energies that seemed to permeate the city itself, as if every stone had been imbued with the enchantments of long-forgotten Aystaran sorcerers.

Jillian, standing beside Aidan, looked just as enraptured by the sight. "I had heard tales of Sunhold's magnificence, but to see it with my own eyes is... beyond words," she murmured.

Ahlissa, guiding the airship as it descended, smiled knowingly. "Sunhold is not just a city; it's the Aystar's soul made manifest. The temples, the libraries, the way it blends seamlessly into the mountain; all of it reflects their commitment to knowledge and legacy."

As the Zephyr Breeze finally docked, they were greeted by the soft, resonant chimes of Sunhold's bells. Their tones were low and melodic, a welcoming sound that seemed to carry a message of peace and wisdom. Aidan felt a deep stirring within him, an almost instinctual sense of belonging he hadn't felt anywhere else. This city, with its awe-inspiring splendour and aura of history, was more than a mere destination. It was a part of him.

The landing platforms were bustling with Aystaran citizens, their regal, finely crafted robes flowing gracefully as they moved with purpose. Some carried books or scrolls, while others bore ceremonial staffs embedded with gemstones that emitted soft glows. A group of elders, dressed in silver-trimmed robes, approached the Zephyr Breeze, their expressions warm yet dignified. They were Keepers of the Past, guardians of Sunhold's knowledge and traditions. Their presence alone was a testament to the city's importance, as they rarely ventured from their posts within the sacred chambers of the temples or libraries.

Aidan and his companions disembarked, bowing respectfully to the Keepers. The advisor Vyrethen, who had accompanied them from Gideon City, introduced the group to the eldest, Shaevath Tyrathalas, a man of tall, slender build with hair as silver as the moonlight, who stepped forward, his gaze resting on Aidan with piercing intensity.

"Welcome to Sunhold," he said, his voice deep and resonant, like the chiming of the ancient bells that had welcomed them. "It is an honour to receive one who has travelled so far to reconnect with the knowledge of our people."

He greeted them warmly but with a solemn air, understanding the gravity of their discovery; the bones of King Thalendir, a long-lost Kale Khestari king whose remains had been retrieved from the shattered Sun Tower in the Tahnaar Desert in Syrnadar.

As they moved through the city's streets, Shaevath guided them with reverent purpose. The thoroughfares were lined with statues of revered Aystaran ancestors, each carved in lifelike detail. Their eyes seemed to follow the newcomers, an effect intensified by the faint Aethyr glow embedded in the statues' pupils. Grand archways adorned with intricate mosaics and precious stones rose over the main roads, creating patterns of light that danced across the stones as they passed. The very air felt different, charged with an ancient power that had seeped into every corner of Sunhold.

They passed a particularly magnificent structure, the Temple of the Ages, its columns carved to resemble ancient trees reaching toward the sky. "The temple holds our most sacred relics," Shaevath explained, sensing Aidan's curiosity. "It is here that we preserve the memories of our ancestors, their wisdom and experiences, all passed down through our rituals. You will be welcome here, should you wish to seek guidance. This is where we will honour the return of King Thalendir's remains."

Aidan nodded, unable to speak from the weight of reverence and awe. He felt as if he was walking within a living chronicle, each building, statue, and artefact a silent witness to the struggles and triumphs of his people. The Keepers of the Past, he realised, were not only scholars but stewards of an entire civilization's memory.

Eventually, they reached the Library of Ancients, its towering doors inscribed with symbols and glyphs from a dozen ancient dialects. The

Library emanated an aura of silence and respect, as if even the stones themselves held their breath in the presence of such vast knowledge. Shaevath paused, gesturing toward the entrance.

"This is the Library of Ancients, where the knowledge of our people is kept safe," he said solemnly. "You will find that Sunhold is not merely a city but a living repository of Aystaran history. It is here that your journey truly begins, Aidan."

Aidan felt a sense of destiny wash over him as he stepped forward. He understood, with sudden clarity, that Sunhold held answers to questions he had not yet dared to ask. This journey to Kharadia was more than just a search for his heritage; it was a path to uncovering a part of himself that had been lost to time. And here, amidst the towering temples, sacred artifacts, and ageless wisdom of the Aystar, he knew he would find it.

"This is no small feat," Shaevath said, his voice resonant with emotion. "For centuries, King Thalendir's lineage was thought to be lost, a mere whisper of history buried beneath the sands of time."

The ceremony to return King Thalendir's bones to the Temple of the Ages was planned quickly. Word spread across the Aystaran lands, reaching even the most distant and scattered factions. Many returned to Sunhold, driven by the need to witness the return of their king's remains and the restoration of an essential part of their history. For the Aystaran people, this was a pivotal moment; both a time of mourning for the loss of their king and a celebration of the rediscovery of their ancient lineage.

The Temple of the Ages itself was a grand structure, a marvel of

Aystaran architecture. Its towering spires reached toward the sky, adorned with carvings depicting the history of the Kale Khestari and the Aystaran people. Inside, the temple was a labyrinth of sacred halls, each dedicated to different aspects of their culture; history, magic, and the divine. The ceremony took place in the central hall, a vast chamber lit by thousands of floating, glowing orbs of light that filled the space with a soft, golden glow.

Aidan, Ahlissa, and Jillian stood among the honoured guests at the ceremony, their presence acknowledged by the entire city. King Iaeras I, the current ruler of the Aystaran people, personally greeted them, his deep blue eyes filled with gratitude.

"You have restored the soul of this land," the king said as he clasped Aidan's hands. "Your discovery is not just one of bones and relics but of who we are. For that, we are eternally in your debt."

Aidan felt the weight of the king's words and the gaze of the assembled crowd. The honour of his discovery and the significance of the moment resonated deeply within him, but he also felt a sense of unease. The past had been uncovered, but what future would it now shape?

The ceremony itself was a spectacle of ancient tradition. The bones of King Thalendir were carried into the central hall by an honour guard, each step reverberating with the weight of history. Shaevath Tyrathalas led the procession, chanting in the ancient Aystaran tongue, his voice echoing off the stone walls. Priests in deep red robes flanked the procession, carrying ornate relics and symbols of Aystar heritage, while the gathered people watched in hushed reverence.

The bones were placed on an elaborately carved altar, its surface inlaid with gold and silver filigree that depicted the rise of the Kale Khestari kings. As Shaevath performed the sacred rites, the air seemed to hum with energy. The assembled crowd of Aystar, and other allied factions stood silent, their collective history binding them together in this pivotal moment.

The solemn silence broke with a surge of song; an ancient hymn that had not been sung in generations. The voices of thousands filled the hall, their tones rising in unison, reverberating through the stone walls and out into the streets of Sunhold. The hymn told of the Kale Khestari kings, their battles, their triumphs, and their sacrifices, and it brought tears to the eyes of many present.

For Aidan, this ceremony wasn't just about returning bones; it was about returning identity, restoring something sacred that had been forgotten by time. He could feel the power of the place, the weight of his bloodline pressing down on him, urging him to uncover more of his heritage. He knew there were still mysteries left to solve, answers buried in the ancient tomes and stone-carved histories of his people.

After the ceremony concluded, King Iaeras I hosted a banquet in honour of Aidan, Ahlissa, and Jillian. The grand dining hall of the palace was filled with the best the Aystaran people could offer; platters of exotic meats, fragrant stews, and delicate pastries were laid out for the guests. Musicians played soft, harmonious tunes, creating a serene backdrop to the celebration.

Amid the festivities, Ahlissa found Aidan in a quieter corner of the hall. She approached him with her usual confident stride, but there was a note of seriousness in her voice. "Aidan, I have new tasks that will take me away for some time," she said. "You'll be safe here in Sunhold.

This is the perfect opportunity for you to learn everything you've ever wanted about the Aystar and your bloodline. But I won't be able to stay."

Aidan, feeling both the excitement of discovery and the sudden absence of his trusted friend, nodded. "I understand. Thank you for bringing me here. It's been... a lot to take in, but I'm glad I came."

Ahlissa's expression softened. "You'll be alright. I know you're strong, and this place holds a lot of answers for you. Don't let the weight of the past overwhelm you. You're not alone."

He smiled slightly, appreciating her words. "I'll manage. I think there's a lot more to discover here than I ever expected."

Ahlissa's eyes gleamed with her usual adventurous spark. "I'm sure there is. I'll be off with the Zephyr Breeze, but if you ever need me, you know where to find me."

As Ahlissa prepared to leave, Jillian approached Aidan. The Khystar shapeshifter had been a close companion throughout their travels, and her decision surprised him.

"I've decided to stay with Ahlissa," Jillian said, her tone thoughtful. "The adventures with her and the crew of the Zephyr Breeze have given me something I hadn't expected; freedom. There's no judgement against me aboard the ship, no scrutinizing eyes of The Thirteen or the prejudices of Gideon City. It's the first time in a long time that I feel like I can breathe."

Aidan nodded, understanding her decision. "You've been a great companion, Jillian. You should follow your heart. It seems like you've found a place where you belong."

Jillian smiled, her eyes reflecting a deep sense of relief. "I think I have. But if you ever need me, just send word. We've been through too much together for me to just disappear from your life."

Aidan smiled in return, but there was a bittersweet quality to it. He knew Jillian was right to pursue her newfound freedom, but he would miss her presence. She had become a valuable friend and ally.

With Ahlissa and Jillian departing, Aidan was left alone in Sunhold. He could feel the weight of history pressing down on him as he stood in the grand halls of the city's ancient temples. The libraries beckoned to him, filled with untold knowledge of the Kale Khestari kings and the secrets of the Aystaran people. It was time for him to begin a new chapter in his life, one that would take him deeper into the mysteries of his bloodline and the ancient power that still resonated through his veins.

The first few weeks in Sunhold were a whirlwind of discovery. Aidan spent his days in the libraries, pouring over old tomes and scrolls, learning everything he could about the Aystaran people and the legacy of the Kale Khestari. His nights were filled with dreams; visions of ancient battles, forgotten gods, and a world long lost to time.

But the deeper he delved into the history of his people, the more he realised that the past was not as distant as he had once thought. The forces that had shaped the Aystar and Khystar in ages past still lingered, hidden in the shadows of the present, waiting for the right moment to emerge once more.

One evening, as Aidan walked through the gardens of the temple, he found himself reflecting on the ceremony, on the significance of King Thalendir's return. The discovery of the king's remains had rekindled a sense of pride and unity among the Aystar, but it had also raised new questions. What else had been lost to time? What other secrets were waiting to be uncovered?

Jillian's words echoed in his mind; "*Would you like me to stay around?*"

He had been so focused on his studies, on the artifacts, that he hadn't truly thought about how much her companionship had meant to him. Jillian had been a steady presence, a friend who understood the weight of history and the burden of expectations. He wished she could have stayed, but he also knew that her path lay elsewhere.

As the weeks passed, Aidan found himself feeling increasingly drawn to the past, not just as a scholar but as someone connected to it in ways he had never fully understood. He could feel the pull of the ancient knowledge he sought, a power that seemed to resonate within him, calling him to unlock the secrets of his bloodline.

In Kharadia, the Temple of the Ages stood as a bastion of knowledge, its grand halls filled with the histories and legends of the Khestar, the progenitors of the Aystaran people. Aidan spent his days poring over texts and ancient relics, discovering that his mother's bloodline was far more distinguished than he had ever imagined. She was a direct descendant of the Khestar voyagers, an ancient sect of explorers who had traversed the Eternal Void to settle on Scylla, bringing with them the seeds of Aystar civilization.

The Khestar had been masters of harnessing and manipulating Aethyr, an ancient and powerful magic that had allowed them to build vast empires and incredible technologies, some of which still lingered in the relics scattered across the known world. But, like many great civilizations, they were divided; split into factions aligned with the powers of light and darkness. Aidan's ancestors, the Kale Khestari, had faced their own internal conflicts, battles that had shaped the history of their people and the worlds they had come to inhabit.

In time, Aidan learned that descendants of his mother's ancestral bloodline had left the Aystar homelands in Kharadia to venture across what would become the Tahnaar Desert in Syrnadar. While many scholars believed that these Aystar had been exiled, Aidan uncovered a different truth. They had left by choice. They were not exiles but warriors; the Kale Khestari, a mercenary force seeking honour and glory by engaging in battle with the ancient Argar Empire and the Zar'tul people. The Kale Khestari had become conquerors, seizing the lands of their enemies and establishing their own ancient kingdom under the rule of King Thalendir.

The discovery weighed heavily on Aidan. He had unearthed the remains of King Thalendir and repatriated them to the Aystar homeland, but now he realised the full significance of that act. The Kale Khestari had not merely been fighters; they were the architects of a new kingdom, one that had stood proudly against the ancient Argar and left a lasting impact on the desert. And now, the remnants of that kingdom still survived, a nomadic faction that worshipped their ancestors with a fervour that bordered on fanaticism.

The nomads held fiercely to their heritage, willing to die in battle to honour the memory of their fallen ancestors. Their fanaticism was not unlike that of their forebears, who had died in the sands to wrest control of the land from the Argar empire. To them, Aidan was an outsider, a scholar with no place among their warrior ranks. But they could not deny his bloodline, and this forced them to offer him a path to acceptance; though the challenge was steep.

Aidan received mentoring from the venerable Shaevath Tyrathalas in the Temple of the Ages. Shaevath was a wise man, deeply connected to the ancient traditions of the Aystaran people, and his teachings resonated with Aidan's scholarly nature. Under Shaevath's guidance, Aidan studied the unaligned faith known as The Spirits of the Past. It was a philosophy that valued tradition, honour, and the wisdom of those who had come before. It called on its followers to look to history for strength and guidance and to emulate the great deeds of their ancestors.

"Remember the great deeds and people of the past," Shaevath would say, "and try to emulate or even surpass them. Nothing is true today that wasn't true in the past; it just wears different trappings."

Aidan absorbed these teachings like a sponge. He had always been drawn to history, but now, it felt personal. His bloodline was tied to the great stories of his people, and his journey was becoming a reflection of those ancient struggles for power, identity, and survival.

Yet, Shaevath's teachings alone could not protect him. The Kale Khestari, the war clans of the desert, viewed Aidan with suspicion. He had the blood of their ancestors, yes, but he was a scholar, not a warrior. And in their eyes, blood alone was not enough. To be accepted by them, he would have to prove his worth in combat; a prospect that Aidan, despite his growing connection to his heritage, dreaded.

Lorian Tyraleth, a stern and accomplished war band leader, took Aidan under his wing as a martial lore tutor. Lorian had little patience for

Aidan's scholarly ways. In his eyes, the desert bred warriors, not bookworms. Aidan had to earn his place among the Kale Khestari, and Lorian made no secret of his doubt that Aidan would survive the trials ahead.

"Become one of us by training as one of us and prove your worth and strength to the Kale Khestari," Lorian had told him. "Do this, and we will accept you. Fail, and we will disown you."

The training was brutal. Lorian pushed Aidan to his physical limits, demanding that he learn the ways of the Kale Khestari warriors; horse riding, swordsmanship, archery, and survival in the harsh desert landscape. Aidan, who had always relied on his intellect, now found himself facing challenges that required endurance, strength, and the will to survive.

For weeks, Aidan endured the gruelling training. Every day, his muscles ached, his body felt battered, and his mind was weighed down by the expectations of the war clans. But he did not give up. The spirits of the past, the ancestors who had once fought for the very sands beneath his feet, spurred him on. He couldn't fail; not when he had come so far in discovering his heritage, not when his ancestors' honour was at stake.

When the time came for the final trials, Aidan was ready. The Kale Khestari gathered in a sacred circle, watching as Aidan took part in the warrior combat and horse-riding trials. The desert sun beat down on him as he faced his opponents, his war horse beneath him, his sword in hand. The combat was fierce, the stakes high. But with every strike, every manoeuvre, Aidan fought with a determination that had grown from both the wisdom of the past and the fire of the present.

In the end, Aidan passed the trials. His acceptance into the ranks of the Kale Khestari was not just a matter of blood; it was a matter of honour. The war clan warriors, once sceptical, now regarded him with respect. He was no longer just a scholar; he was one of them. Aidan's journey had transformed him, bridging the gap between his scholarly past and the warrior spirit of his ancestors.

As Aidan continued his studies in Kharadia, he became increasingly intrigued by the old maps and texts that spoke of the Aystar's ancient battles against the Argar Empire. He spent long nights in the library, pouring over forgotten records and examining the locations of ancient fortresses and guard towers that had once stood as sentinels during the ten-thousand-year-old conflict. His mind raced with the possibilities, wondering what secrets still lay buried beneath the desert sands.

3

The Long Patrol

The Temple of the Ages was a sacred place, its architecture designed to inspire awe and reverence in all who entered. Aidan stood in silent contemplation beneath the high vaulted ceiling, carved from alabaster and soaring above him. The delicate arches and intricately carved stone pillars around the circular chamber spoke of a time when artistry and devotion to the ancestors were intertwined. Soft shafts of light filtered through the temple's windows, casting faint, golden patterns upon the stone floor.

For a moment, Aidan marvelled at the craftsmanship. It was hard not to be moved by the beauty of the temple, but his thoughts quickly drifted back to the heavy burden that had followed him since childhood; the uncertainty of his parentage and the violent mystery of their deaths. As he stood there in deep reflection, the quiet murmurs of four adepts sitting on the far side of the chamber occasionally broke the silence, though their voices seemed distant and removed from his inner turmoil.

Aidan had always struggled with his place in the world. The Kale Khestari warriors, with their fierce pride and ancient traditions, regarded him with suspicion. He was a scholar among warriors, an outsider among a people bound by blood and battle. The knowledge of his ancestry eluded him, and without knowing the name of his direct ancestor, he felt a profound emptiness. This uncertainty made it difficult to find his place, especially among the Kale Khestari who valued lineage and martial prowess above all else.

The warriors of the Kale Khestari viewed him as weak, and Aidan knew it. They did not see him as one of their own. Their derision cut deep, and the void within him only grew as he realised, he didn't know who to honour or whose memory to uphold. It troubled him, this lack of connection to the past, and it gnawed at his sense of identity.

Soft footsteps echoed behind him, breaking his reverie. A familiar voice, calm and reassuring, spoke gently.

"Are you troubled today, Aidan?" asked Shaevath Tyrathalas. He was dressed in his plain, flowing sand-coloured robes, his soft leather sandals barely making a sound as he approached.

Aidan turned to face Shaevath and offered a faint smile. "A little," he admitted. "I think about the past often, and I wonder about the future."

"Do not be troubled," Shaevath said, his voice filled with compassion. "You are still young, with much to learn of our ways. You were lost to us for many years but know this; the ancestors have kindly delivered you back to your homeland. Their spirits watch over you, as they do over all of us. In time, they will reveal the name of your ancestor. The longer you stay with us, the stronger your bond will grow. You belong here, with us."

Aidan nodded, his heart slightly lightened by the elder's words. He knew Shaevath spoke the truth, but the void in his soul remained.

"I thank you for your guidance, Master Tyrathalas," Aidan replied softly, bowing his head in respect.

Shaevath gave him a warm smile before his tone shifted to one of instruction. "The war clans are preparing for new long-range patrols. Lorian Tyraleth has informed me that you will accompany his group to further your training. He is right in this matter, Aidan. I understand your fondness for research and study, but the spirits of our ancestors have spoken through him. You must continue to train with the war clans. Go now and prepare yourself. Gather what you need from the Peasants' Market and report to War clan Tyraleth's marquee within the hour."

Aidan sighed inwardly but nodded. He was grateful for Shaevath's mentorship, but the call to war still felt foreign to him. He longed for the quietness of books and maps, for the comfort of ancient texts. But the Kale Khestari way was not his own, and the expectations of the Kale Khestari weighed heavily on his shoulders. He bowed once more to Shaevath, then exited the temple, heading toward the market to prepare for the coming patrol.

The Peasants' Market was a bustling, dusty hub of activity. Traders and merchants called out to passers-by, their voices competing with the clamour of bartering and haggling. The smell of fresh spices, grilled meat, and baked bread filled the air, mixing with the dust kicked up by hundreds of boots and hooves. The marketplace was chaotic, and Aidan could see traders physically grabbing potential customers as they tried to pull them toward their stalls. Despite the hustle and bustle, the merchants knew better than to overcharge today; the war clans were preparing to leave, and they did not want to jeopardize future business with inflated prices.

Aidan moved through the crowd, gathering the supplies he needed for the journey. His interactions were brief, the traders recognising that he was in a hurry. They offered him fair prices, knowing that the war clans held sway over much of the city's commerce, and cheating one of their own could result in severe consequences.

As Aidan moved through the market, he observed the crowd around him. It struck him that very few Aystar conducted their own business here. The Kale Khestari were aloof, dismissive of the mundane tasks associated with trade. Instead, they sent their servants - peasants and labourers from conquered lands - to handle these affairs. For most Aystar, the market was beneath them, a place of foreign visitors, adventurers, and new migrants, not a place for the proud Kale Khestari.

Despite his growing acceptance into Kale Khestari society, Aidan knew he was still seen as an outsider by many. His mixed blood and scholarly ways set him apart, and his presence in the market, though familiar to him, was unusual for one aspiring to be fully accepted by the Kale Khestari war clans.

As he scanned the market, Aidan noticed a group of Argar maintaining a secure perimeter around a rather large, overweight Argar shaman. The Argar were tense, distrustful of anyone who came too close. Their shields bore the symbol of a clawed fist with an open eye in the centre, an unfamiliar heraldry to Aidan. This wasn't surprising; new factions and groups arrived on the frontier all the time, and the market was a melting pot for such strange allegiances.

At another stall, Aidan saw three finely dressed scholars, each wearing dark robes with gray vests and boots. Their belts bore the insignia of the Mhargrave Outreach Society. They were deeply engaged in a conversation with a cartographer, who seemed to be struggling to convince them of the accuracy of his maps. Aidan surmised these were likely field students from Mhargrave University, backed by considerable funding. Their presence was no coincidence; that Adeni faction had always had an interest in the region's history and ruins.

Distracted momentarily, Aidan caught sight of an Adeni belly dancer performing nearby. Her movements were fluid and mesmerizing, her exotic appearance drawing the attention of a growing crowd. For a moment, Aidan found himself captivated by her grace, but he quickly shook himself free of the distraction. She had drawn quite a crowd, and the coins thrown at her feet were watched over by a suspicious-looking Argar who scowled at anyone who ventured too close.

Moving through the crowd, Aidan deftly avoided a group of roguish individuals who lingered near the edges of the market. He knew well the dangers of the Peasants' Market; pickpockets operated freely here, knowing that the city's justice system turned a blind eye to minor crimes within its chaotic centre. Kale Khestari justice was swift and brutal, but it was also highly selective. The Peasants' Market was its own little world, a place where the rules were bent and sometimes broken.

Having gathered what he needed, Aidan made his way to War clan Tyraleth's marquee, arriving just before the hour. The war clan's sentries stood at attention outside the entrance, their eyes cold as they regarded Aidan. After a brief pause, they ushered him inside.

The interior of the marquee was spacious and cool, a welcome respite from the heat outside. Thick woven mats had been laid out across the sand, and the clan members sat comfortably on large cushions. The scent of incense filled the air, and a light breeze passed through the flapping canvas, bringing with it a sense of calm before the upcoming patrol.

Aidan noticed the odd stares from some of the warriors as he entered. Despite his training, he was still regarded as an outsider, a scholar among soldiers. After a few moments, a group of warriors made room for him near the edge of the gathering, brusquely motioning for him to sit.

He settled onto one of the thick mats, feeling the eyes of the others on him. A young half-Aystar seated beside him looked up and offered a faint smile.

"I am Tiralas," the warrior introduced himself. "You must be Aidan. It is good to see you have rejoined us. Many of my brothers had their doubts about you, but I did not. Look," Tiralas motioned to the centre of the marquee. "Lorian is about to address us. We should stand to show respect."

The marquee fell silent as Lorian Tyraleth stepped forward, raising his arms in a gesture for silence. The clan leader's presence commanded attention. He was a warrior through and through, his gaze sharp and his posture straight.

"My brothers, my warriors," Lorian began, his voice carrying across the marquee, "we have gathered here to honour our ancestors and to complete the ritual of brotherhood before we set out once more into the harsh sands. This patrol will test us all. It will test our resolve, our faith, and our determination to defend our homeland against those who would seek to steal it."

The warriors nodded in approval, some offering quiet cheers.

"We will champion the memory of our ancestors," Lorian continued. "We will carry their honour with us as we ride across the unforgiving sands. Our initial patrol will take us west, to our fortified outpost at Kaldorin."

Aidan listened intently as Lorian and the commanders outlined the expectations for the journey. Nothing out of the ordinary was mentioned, though the patrol would be long and arduous, taking them deep into the desert.

At the conclusion of the briefing, the warriors stood and began to file out of the marquee. Aidan moved with the others, gathering his belongings and preparing to ride. He felt a sense of unease settling in his stomach. Though he had trained for this, there was still a part of him that longed for the safety of the Temple of the Ages, where books and knowledge, not swords and shields, were his companions.

The war clan, two hundred strong, rode westward from Kale Khaestas, leaving behind the fertile lands and riding hard for six hours until they reached the broken lands beyond. Aidan rode near the back of the column, watching as the desert began to stretch out before them, a sea of endless sand and jagged rock.

Eventually, the war band came to a halt near the entrance to a small ravine. The sun was beginning to set, casting long shadows across the landscape. Aidan was summoned to the head of the column, where

Lorian awaited him.

"I have a task for you, Aidan," Lorian said. "I want you to scout ahead through the ravine. Take Tiralas with you. Report back when you reach the end."

Aidan nodded, accepting the assignment. He was ready; at least, he hoped he was.

As the war band set up camp, Aidan and Tiralas rode forward into the ravine, the walls of rock towering above them. The path twisted and turned through the narrow passage, the sound of their horses' hooves echoing off the stone. The air grew cooler, the light of the setting sun barely reaching the ground as the shadows lengthened.

As they rode, Tiralas spoke quietly. "Some of the others say you are like a newborn foal, lost and unsure. But I see differently. I think you've come home, Aidan. You just haven't realised it yet."

Aidan considered his words, but the doubt remained. "I'll never feel at home until I know who my parents were," he admitted.

Tiralas nodded. "Perhaps. But the spirits of our ancestors will reveal themselves in time. You are one of us, whether you realize it or not."

They rode in silence for a time before Tiralas suddenly halted, his eyes narrowing as he motioned for Aidan to stop. "Listen," he whispered.

Aidan strained to hear, his senses heightened. There was a faint slithering sound, like something scraping against the rock. He reached for the hilt of his sword as Tiralas readied his bow.

"Move forward quietly," Tiralas commanded, his voice barely audible.

Aidan dismounted and crept forward, his heart pounding in his chest. With a determined gesture, he summoned the Aethyr to cast a quietening spell on his boots, producing enough silence to muffle his footsteps as he approached the curve in the path.

Suddenly, a flash of movement caught his eye; a dark green, reptilian shape sliding swiftly into a nearby cave. Aidan's pulse quickened. He gestured to Tiralas, who was already nocking an arrow.

Two large serpent-like creatures had disappeared into the cave, their presence confirmed by the strange tracks in the dirt.

Tiralas joined him, his face grim. "Those tracks ... could be Zar'tul," he said quietly. "If they've regrouped, we're in trouble."

4

The Guard Post of Athosin

After cautiously navigating the ravine's winding, rocky path, the landscape began to change. The towering cliffs slowly gave way to rolling hills and patches of arid grasslands, where sparse tufts of dry, yellowed vegetation clung to life. The air felt lighter as the ravine opened, and a sense of relief washed over Aidan. He cast a glance at Tiralas, who seemed focused and alert despite the long ride.

In the distance, the small stone tower of Athosin rose above the hills, surrounded by a few modest outbuildings. The structures, though weathered by the elements, appeared functional; outposts for the watchers who patrolled these lands. Aidan squinted, trying to discern any signs of movement, but saw none. His unease, which had been lingering since their encounter with the serpent creatures, only deepened.

"That will be the guard post of Athosin," Tiralas said, his tone measured but tinged with caution. "Aside from our little encounter, the way appears clear. I want to contact the watchers and ensure all is well, then we will ride back to inform Lorian of what we've sighted."

Aidan nodded in agreement, though he shared Tiralas's concern. Something about the quietness of the outpost felt off. There should have been sentries posted at the perimeter, some sign of life. Yet, as they approached, the outpost remained silent.

The outbuildings - a grain store, a barracks, and a utility hall - were clustered at the base of a small hill, with the tower standing just 15 feet above them. The hill wasn't particularly steep, but the tower gave the defenders a strategic vantage point over the surrounding terrain. Still, no one greeted them as they drew closer. No watchful eyes peered down from the tower, no guards stood ready with their weapons at hand.

"This is troubling," Tiralas muttered, his voice low. "We should be warmly greeted, yet we stand here unacknowledged. Something is wrong."

Aidan scanned the area, his instincts on high alert. His sharp eyes caught a glimpse of something; movement behind the utility hall, a shadow that flickered out of sight just as he turned his head. He pointed to the far side of the building, where he thought he'd seen the figure.

Tiralas followed Aidan's gaze and pulled out an eyeglass, inspecting the area from where they stood. After a moment, he lowered it, shaking his head. "I see nothing from here," he said grimly. "We can either move closer to investigate or leave and report back. What do you suggest?"

Aidan reached into his saddlebag and pulled out a pair of glasses, slipping them over his eyes. With the enchanted lenses, he surveyed the buildings again, looking for hidden threats or illusions. Yet, even with the enhanced vision, he saw nothing unusual.

"We should move closer," Aidan said finally, the unease growing heavier in his gut. He didn't like the silence. The air felt thick, as if something dangerous lingered just out of sight. "But cautiously."

Tiralas nodded, his expression grim. He had already unslung his long-bow, holding it at the ready as they advanced toward the outbuildings, their footsteps muffled by the soft sand beneath them.

As they neared the grain store, Aidan noticed strange markings in the sand; snake trails, winding and curving across the ground. Some of the trails were small, but others were wide and deep, as though something large had slithered through recently. He knelt to inspect the tracks more closely, tracing them with his fingers.

"There are at least ten of them," Aidan said quietly. "And one of them is very large."

Tiralas crouched beside him, examining the trails with a furrowed brow. "These are fresh," he muttered, his voice tense. "A large snake trail like this could mean that a Zar'tul warrior is nearby. It would be the leader of the group and likely very powerful. They are masters of camouflage and deception; they could already be surrounding us if they're still here."

Aidan's hand tightened around the hilt of his sword. His eyes scanned the open ground, and he felt a chill run down his spine. This was no ordinary outpost. The Zar'tul, if they were here, were far more dangerous than any bandits or wild creatures.

"We're exposed out here," Tiralas said, his voice steady but urgent. "Let's get closer to some cover. Follow me."

Tiralas darted toward the nearest outbuilding - the grain store - and vaulted over the low wooden fence that marked the perimeter of the guard post. Aidan followed, his heart pounding in his chest. They crouched low behind the grain store, peering around the corner toward the utility hall, where Aidan had first seen movement.

"Good," Tiralas whispered, keeping his bow at the ready. "Now I want you to make your way to the utility hall. I'll cover you. Crouch by the door, and once you're there, I'll join you."

Aidan nodded, his palms slick with sweat as he gripped his sword. He could feel the tension in the air, the weight of impending danger. With a deep breath, he darted from behind the grain store, sprinting across the open ground and crouching by the utility hall's door. Tiralas's eyes never left him, his longbow aimed and ready to fire at any sign of movement.

Aidan pressed his back against the wooden door, his breaths shallow and quick. He glanced inside through a small window but saw nothing; no movement, no signs of life. He waited as Tiralas approached, his longbow at the ready, before the young warrior joined him at the door.

"There's no movement inside," Aidan whispered.

Tiralas nodded, shouldering his bow and drawing his longsword. He murmured a word in Aystar, and the blade glowed with an icy frost, a chill emanating from its edge. "Let's go," he said, pushing open the door and stepping inside.

The air inside the utility hall was thick with the scent of death.

Aidan and Tiralas found themselves in what must have once been the dining hall of the outpost. Now, it was a scene of carnage. Plates, cups, and utensils were scattered across the floor, some shattered, others stained with blood. Several large wooden tables had been overturned and arranged in a makeshift barricade near the far corner of the room. Behind the barricade were the bodies of six Kale Khestari warriors, their lifeless forms pierced by arrows with red and green fletching. Some had died from close-quarters combat, their bodies bearing deep slashing wounds.

Tiralas's face darkened with fury as he took in the sight of his fallen brothers. "They were eating when they were attacked," he said through gritted teeth. "Cowards. The Zar'tul took them by surprise."

Near the window, another Kale Khestari warrior lay face down, a pool of blood spreading beneath him. He had been struck down by a vicious slashing blow, likely from a bladed weapon. His hand still clutched the hilt of his sword, as though he had tried to defend himself in his final moments.

Aidan's stomach churned at the sight. He had seen death before, but this was different. These warriors had been caught off guard, ambushed in their place of rest. It was a dishonourable, brutal end for men who deserved better.

The low archway at the back of the dining hall led into the relaxation room, where more blood and destruction awaited. Two more bodies lay in ruin, one slumped forward in his chair with an arrow protruding from his back, while the other appeared to have fought ferociously before falling. Dark, viscous blood trailed from his body, leading outside.

Tiralas crouched by the blood trail, his expression grim. "My brothers fought bravely, but the enemy struck first. There is hope, though' this blood is not theirs. One of the Zar'tul must have been wounded. Their blood will lead us to them."

Suddenly, Aidan's ears picked up the faint sound of stones skittering against wood; the sound of movement above them, on the wooden steps leading up to the watchtower. His senses sharpened, and he turned his gaze to the tower. Something was up there, lurking, watching.

Tiralas moved to a window, crouching low and peering out. "There are two figures up there," he said quietly. "They don't look like Aystar. They could be Adeni, but..." He trailed off, his eyes narrowing. "No. They're not Adeni. They're speaking in a hissing tongue."

Aidan's blood ran cold. "Zar'tul shifters," he whispered. "They appear Adeni, but they're not. They're the weakest of their kind, but they won't be alone."

Tiralas nodded, his face set with grim determination. "We'll need to take them by surprise if we're to stand a chance. Stay out of sight."

Aidan moved behind one of the overturned chairs, taking cover. Tiralas concealed himself behind a nearby sofa, both readying their weapons. The air was heavy with tension, and Aidan's pulse quickened as the slow, deliberate footsteps of the Zar'tul descended the tower stairs.

The creatures were close now, their voices low and hissing. Aidan caught a glimpse of a shadow moving near the side entrance of the relaxation room, but it quickly disappeared, the footsteps retreating across the sand toward the barracks.

Tiralas signalled with his hand; a silent command to attack. Aidan nodded, his heart pounding in his chest as he readied his bow. The two shifters moved into view, oblivious to their presence.

Tiralas was the first to act. He rose from his position, his bow drawn, and fired an arrow at the closest Zar'tul shifter. The arrow struck true, sinking into the creature's back. The Zar'tul hissed in pain, spinning around to face its attackers, its discoloured green skin glistening in the light.

Aidan followed Tiralas's lead, firing an arrow of his own at the second enemy. His shot struck the creature in the back, drawing a guttural curse from its lips. Both creatures turned toward them, their eyes glowing with malice.

The first Zar'tul raised its arms, chanting in its hissing tongue. With a motion of its hand, a mass of writhing snakes erupted from the ground at Tiralas's feet. But the Kale Khestari warrior was quick, leaping clear of the vipers as they scattered across the sand.

The second Zar'tul conjured a swirling scimitar of sand, the weapon forming in its hand as it charged forward. Aidan fired another arrow, his heart racing as the Zar'tul closed in, but his shot went wide.

Tiralas dropped his bow and drew his frost-enchanted sword, charging at the first shifter with deadly precision. His blade struck deep, and the Zar'tul staggered, its life draining away as it collapsed to the ground.

The second Zar'tul shifter swung its sand scimitar at Tiralas, but he deftly sidestepped the blow. Aidan, still firing from a distance, loosed another arrow that struck the creature in the chest. Tiralas took advantage of the opening, slashing at the shifter with his frosted blade.

The Zar'tul hissed in pain, but it was far from finished. With a vicious swing of its scimitar, it caught Tiralas across the arm, drawing blood. But Tiralas was undeterred. He retaliated with a powerful strike, cutting deep into the creature's leg.

Aidan fired one final arrow, and it found its mark. The Zar'tul staggered, its breath rattling in its throat as it slumped to the ground, dead.

Breathing heavily, Tiralas quickly rejoined Aidan inside the relaxation room, casting a wary glance at the tower. "There are more of them up there," he said, wiping the blood from his blade. "But we were lucky. We can't take them all. Let's fall back."

Aidan nodded, agreeing that they needed to leave. They had done well to defeat these two, but the outpost was compromised, and reinforcements would be needed to reclaim it.

Together, they made their way back to their horses, the weight of the battle still heavy on their minds. As they mounted, Aidan looked back at the tower one last time, expecting more trouble.

But the tower remained still, though Aidan could feel the eyes of the Zar'tul watching from above.

They rode hard, pushing their horses through the ravine as quickly as they dared. Aidan kept glancing back, half expecting to see the Zar'tul giving chase, but the path behind them remained clear. The poison that had struck Tiralas was beginning to take its toll, but Aidan had managed to delay its effects with his healing spells. Tiralas was cold, his skin pale, but he remained conscious, his willpower keeping him in the saddle.

As they neared the camp, several warriors moved to escort them immediately to Lorian, who furrowed his brow in concern as he saw the state of Tiralas.

"He has been poisoned," Aidan explained quickly. "I've delayed the effects, but he needs proper treatment."

Lorian immediately summoned the healers, who whisked Tiralas away to their tent. Then, he turned to Aidan with a stern but grateful expression.

"Tell me, what has happened?" Lorian asked, his voice steady despite the urgency.

Aidan recounted the events at the outpost, showing Lorian the map and explaining the numbers and positions of the Zar'tul they had encountered. Lorian listened intently, his expression darkening as the details unfolded.

"You have done well to bring this news to me," Lorian said, his voice firm. "Rest now. We will attend to this menace. The guard post of Athosin will be reclaimed."

Lorian wasted no time. Within hours, he gathered fifty warriors and led them into the ravine, determined to purge the Zar'tul from the outpost. Aidan, though weary from the day's events, joined the war band, riding with them as they set out to retake Athosin.

When Aidan arrived back at the guard post, he saw the bodies of the Zar'tul staked out in the sun; a gruesome warning to any others who might dare trespass on Kale Khestari land. The war band had succeeded. The outpost had been reclaimed, and the fallen warriors had been avenged.

As dusk settled over the guard post, a solemn ceremony was held for the fallen Aystaran warriors. Their bodies were laid on a wooden pyre, and songs of honour and remembrance were sung beneath the stars. Aidan stood beside Lorian, watching the flames flicker as the warriors' spirits were returned to the ancestors.

Lorian, his expression a mix of pride and sadness, placed a hand on Aidan's shoulder. "You fought well," he said quietly. "You have earned the respect of your brothers."

He handed Aidan a bracelet; a simple string of blue and red, with a carved wooden falcon attached. "This was made by one of my ancestors. Now, it is yours. It will bring you luck."

Aidan thanked him, feeling the weight of the bracelet in his hand.

"We will camp here for the night," Lorian said, surveying the freshly claimed guard post of Athosin. "In the morning, I will leave twenty warriors to hold this position. The rest of us will ride hard through the day, and we should reach Kaldorin by tomorrow night. Rest now, Aidan. Eat well, regain your strength, and join one of the watch shifts to keep your skills sharp."

Aidan nodded, feeling the fatigue beginning to settle into his bones after the day's events. The adrenaline of battle had left him, and all that remained was a dull ache in his limbs and a gnawing hunger in his stomach. He made his way toward the cooking fires, where the smell of roasting meat filled the air.

He sat down with a few of the warriors, joining them for a quiet meal. Most were deep in their own thoughts, their minds likely on the fallen comrades they had just honoured or the looming uncertainties of their journey ahead. Despite the solemnity of the evening, Aidan felt a sense of belonging that he hadn't expected. Though he had been an outsider among these warriors, today had proven that he could contribute and earn their respect.

Later that night, Aidan was assigned the early watch shift. The desert was eerily quiet, save for the occasional rustle of wind through the sparse vegetation. He kept his eyes sharp, but the night was uneventful, save for the distant howl of a wild animal. As dawn broke, Aidan finished his shift and returned to help the war clan break down camp.

As Aidan was folding up the canvas of the main marquee, Tiralas approached him with a smile. "I wanted to thank you for helping me yesterday," he said. "Without your healing skills, that poison would have claimed my life for sure. You've earned a lot of respect from our brothers because of your actions."

Aidan shrugged modestly, not entirely comfortable with the praise. "I did what I could. I was lucky to have enough knowledge to delay the poison."

Tiralas clapped him on the shoulder. "Luck had nothing to do with it. You knew what to do, and you acted quickly. That's what saved me. Tell me, what other spells can you cast? I'm curious. You seem to have a few surprises up your sleeve."

Aidan smiled faintly. "I can cast a few wizard spells. Not many, though. Most of my magic is more academic; bardic, really. I can decipher texts, enhance knowledge, things like that. More useful in libraries than in battles."

Tiralas raised an eyebrow. "And fighting magic? Can you cast a fireball or something similarly destructive?"

"No, nothing offensive," Aidan admitted. "It's just not in my skillset."

"A pity," Tiralas said, though he smiled. "It would have been useful, but you've done more than enough. Yesterday, I saw how you handled yourself. For someone who prefers books to blades, you did rather well under pressure. Maybe next time, you'll join me in close-quarters combat. I think you'd make a fine warrior."

Aidan laughed nervously, remembering his encounters with enemies in the sands. While he had survived those encounters, they were a far cry from the organised combat of the war clans.

Tiralas caught Aidan's expression and laughed. "Given your inexperience, I'm even more impressed with how well you held your own. Don't worry; being a marksman from a distance isn't a bad thing, but maybe one day you'll stand with me on the frontline."

Aidan wasn't so sure about that, but he appreciated Tiralas 's confidence in him.

The war clan was ready to move out. The morning sun blazed across the sky as the call to arms sounded, and Aidan joined the others in preparing for the ride. He donned his armour and a tunic, its fabric shimmering subtly under the sunlight. The symbol of Velis was emblazoned on the chest; a reminder of the power and danger tied to his recent past.

Lorian, their leader, stood at the head of the column, surveying his warriors. With a nod of approval, he spurred his horse forward, leading the war clan across the barren grassy plains. The landscape was a mixture of dry, cracked earth and sparse patches of tough, wiry grass that clung to life in the arid wasteland. The air was dry, and the sun climbed higher as the day progressed, beating down on them with relentless heat.

They rode for hours, pushing through the unforgiving desert. Aidan kept pace with the others, his thoughts drifting between the battle at Athosin, his ever-growing connection to the war clan, and the mysteries that still lay ahead. The farther they rode from the ravine, the more he could feel the weight of his own destiny tugging at him.

As the hours passed, the war clan descended into the vast sandy wastelands. The fertile lands behind them vanished, and the world around them became a sea of dunes and barren, sun-scorched plains. The occasional rocky outcrop broke the horizon, but for the most part, they rode through an endless expanse of shifting sands, until they reached the outer edges of Kaldorin.

5

Kaldorin

The war clan pulled their horses to a stop, taking in the sight before them. Lorian gestured for his warriors to spread out and search the immediate area for any signs of danger or activity.

"This is where we will make camp for the night," Lorian announced. "Tomorrow, we will conduct our business here and resupply. There are ruins around Kaldorin that hold many secrets, and it is said that some of those who once ruled here still walk the sands in spirit form."

Aidan's heart skipped a beat at Lorian's words. There was always something about these ruins that felt more than just abandoned buildings. The thought of ancient spirits walking among the stones sent a shiver down his spine, but at the same time, a spark of curiosity ignited within him.

When the camp was settled, and the fire crackled softly in the darkness, Aidan stared out into the vastness of the desert, where the ruins of Kaldorin loomed silently in the distance.

The fortified town of Kaldorin buzzed with activity, a stark contrast to the desolation of the desert plains that stretched endlessly around it. Though small, Kaldorin was a vital military staging post for the Kale Khestari people, its high stone walls and reinforced gates a testament to its strategic importance. Two large war clans made up the local garrison - nearly 400 strong - fierce warriors sworn to defend their lands with their lives. The narrow streets were bustling with soldiers and traders alike, but the air was thick with the quiet tension that always accompanied a place built for war.

Aidan could feel the weight of it pressing down on him, even as he tried to relax. After days of riding through the barren plains and surviving the harrowing encounter with the Zar'tul, the war clan was finally at rest within the safety of Kaldorin's walls. Yet, Aidan's mind raced with thoughts of what lay ahead.

That evening, Lorian attended a high-level meeting with the town's military leaders, discussing plans and strategies. It left Aidan and the rest of the war clan free to rest or enjoy the limited pleasures the town had to offer. Some of the warriors sought out the taverns, eager for ale and good company, while others visited the local merchants to replenish their supplies. But Aidan, as usual, sought the solace of study.

He had found a quiet room at the local inn, a small but cosy space with a window that overlooked the busy street below. His books and scrolls were scattered across the table, illuminated by the soft glow of a lantern. He was lost in thought, poring over an ancient text about the history of the Khestar, trying to uncover more about his elusive ancestry.

Yet even as he studied, he found it difficult to focus. His mind kept drifting to his recent dreams, unsettling visions of shadowy figures watching him, and the strange burning sensation that lingered long after he awoke. The Keepers of the Past had offered no answers, only cryptic warnings that something was stirring. Aidan wasn't sure what it all meant, but he couldn't shake the feeling that it was all connected; his past, his bloodline, the strange power he had tapped into back in Kanarzand.

Suddenly, the familiar sound of an airship passing overhead broke through his thoughts. Curious, Aidan rose from his chair and moved to the window. Peering out, he caught sight of a sleek, silver-blue ship gliding gracefully over the rooftops of Kaldorin.

Aidan's heart leaped at the sight of the ship. He hadn't seen Ahlissa or the crew in quite some time, not since the chaos in Gideon City after the downfall of Kanarzand. For a moment, a sense of nostalgia washed over him, reminding him of the adventures they had shared aboard that airship, high above the desert sands.

The Zephyr Breeze touched down on the far side of the town, docking at the landing platform near the military supply depot. Aidan hesitated for only a moment before deciding he needed a break from his studies. He quickly donned casual clothing, opting for a simple vest and pockets, leaving his weapons locked securely in the room's personal safe. With a final glance at his scattered books, he stepped out into the cool night air.

The streets of Kaldorin were still busy, even as the evening deepened. Soldiers moved through the town in small groups, and the sounds of laughter and conversation drifted from the taverns. Aidan navigated the narrow, winding streets with ease, heading toward the airship platform.

As he neared the platform, he could see the crew of the Zephyr Breeze unloading crates and boxes; military supplies by the look of it. Aidan noticed something curious. Unlike in Gideon City or Kanarzand, where the crew had always worn their face masks to protect themselves from the suspicions of outsiders, here in Kaldorin, they were unmasked. The crew moved about confidently, their Aystar features unmistakable as they worked in the open.

Aidan stood at a distance, watching the scene with interest. He was excited at the thought that Ahlissa was aboard. He had always admired her strength and independence, and he missed their conversations. He was about to turn away when he heard a familiar voice calling his name.

"Aidan!" Ahlissa's voice rang out from above.

Looking up, Aidan saw her standing on the deck of the Zephyr Breeze, waving down at him with a bright smile. She was as striking as ever, her long, silver, blonde hair flowing in the breeze, her armour gleaming under the lantern light. "Come up!" she called, motioning for him to join her.

Aidan felt a rush of warmth at the sight of her. He quickly climbed the steps to the platform, where one of the crew members greeted him and escorted him to the deck of the ship.

When he stepped aboard, Ahlissa was there to greet him, her smile broad and genuine. "Fancy meeting you here, among all these warriors," she said with a teasing lilt to her voice.

Aidan grinned sheepishly, feeling a bit out of place. "Well, I saw your ship and thought I'd try to see you. Or at least leave a note... something like that."

Ahlissa laughed, a musical sound that always seemed to put him at ease. "Ah, yes, that's the Aidan I know. The one who'd rather leave a note than take direct action."

Aidan blushed slightly, rubbing the back of his neck. "You know me too well."

She studied him for a moment, her sharp eyes taking in his appearance. "So, tell me, how's life playing at being a soldier? Do you feel as big and strong as they want you to be?"

Aidan sighed, shaking his head. "Absolutely not. This... this isn't me at all. You know that."

"I figured as much." Ahlissa stepped closer, leaning against the railing as she regarded him with a mixture of amusement and curiosity. "And what about your books? Are you still wrapped up in them, or have they managed to knock that out of you?"

Aidan gave her a wry smile. "How would you like it to be? Would you prefer me as I was, or as they want me to be? Because, as I was, is how you found me. And I managed to do a few things without looking like a warrior."

Ahlissa nodded thoughtfully, her expression softening. "Yes, word has travelled about the 'lost youngling half-Aystar.' The scholar who doesn't know his true heritage. The one who yearns to be complete, to understand his past."

Aidan looked away, feeling a pang of discomfort at her words. "Why is there so much interest in me?" he asked quietly. "I'm not that special."

Ahlissa's gaze remained on him, her voice gentle but firm. "Isn't it obvious? You are something they will never be. They've only ever known battle. They were born and bred for war. The Kale Khestari are an intolerant people, and you... you bring something different. You bring tolerance where it shouldn't exist. You've experienced the other side; you've witnessed prejudice. The Keepers of the Past believe your rejoining your lost brothers is no coincidence. They think it's meant to be."

Aidan frowned, unsure of what to say.

Ahlissa continued, her voice steady. "The tests you've endured to be accepted by us, your people, have proven you're worthy. It doesn't matter what any warrior says about you. They can't deny that you are one of them."

She paused, her eyes narrowing slightly. "But there's one who still won't accept you; my fiancé, Ivistar. He makes that very clear."

Aidan sighed inwardly at the mention of Ivistar. He had never liked the arrogant warlord, but he had done his best to stay out of his way.

"Ivistar calls you an 'outsider,'" Ahlissa said, her tone tinged with frustration. "He doesn't believe it's possible for someone like you to belong to the Kale Khestari. I find him tedious in this matter, and there will come a time when he'll have to acknowledge you. That time might come far sooner than he realises."

Aidan hesitated before speaking. "Look, I don't really care about his acknowledgment. I just want our friendship to remain as it is. I hope his issues don't get in the way of that."

Ahlissa smiled at him, a playful glint in her eyes. "Why, Aidan, the gentleman and smooth talker. I would never let Ivistar get between us as friends. Never. I'm independently minded, and he knows that. So do you."

Aidan smiled, feeling a weight lift from his shoulders.

"Tell me," Ahlissa said, stepping closer. "What are your plans for the rest of the evening?"

Aidan shrugged. "I hadn't really thought about it. Just resting, I suppose."

Ahlissa's eyes gleamed with mischief. "How would you like to take a flight across the sands in the Zephyr Breeze? Just like old times?"

Aidan's face lit up. "I'd love to!"

"Then it's settled," Ahlissa said, turning to give orders to her crew. "We'll raise anchor shortly. And while we're flying, there's something I need to discuss with you. In particular... your dreams."

Aidan's heart skipped a beat at her mention of his dreams. He hadn't told many people about them, but it seemed Ahlissa knew more than she was letting on.

As the crew prepared the ship for flight, Aidan couldn't help but feel a surge of excitement. The familiar hum of the engines, the cool breeze of the night, and the sense of adventure that always accompanied their flights together; this was where he felt most at home.

6

A Dangerous Mark

The Zephyr Breeze weighed anchor, its propulsion systems humming to life as the sleek airship drifted away from the platform above Kaldorin, moving out across the darkened plains toward the low hills silhouetted on the horizon. The air was crisp, and the desert below seemed like an endless sea of shadows. Inside the ship, the crew worked with their usual quiet efficiency, attending to their duties on the bridge and deck. They had donned their face masks once more, a precaution against the wasteland's ever-present wind-blown sand and debris.

Aidan stood on the deck, watching the vast expanse below them with a mix of anticipation and uncertainty. It had been a long time since he had flown with Ahlissa aboard the Zephyr Breeze, and as much as he enjoyed the freedom of the skies, there was an underlying tension he couldn't shake.

After a brief flight of about half an hour, Ahlissa commanded the crew to halt the airship. They hovered above a series of dark hills, far from the bustle and prying eyes of Kaldorin.

Ahlissa stepped up beside him, pointing across the landscape. "It's safe to speak here," she said softly, her voice carried by the desert breeze. "Tell me more about your dreams."

Aidan glanced at her, his brow furrowing. "What do you mean 'safe to speak here'? Was it not safe to speak in the city?"

Ahlissa smiled faintly, though her eyes were serious. "Perhaps. But who truly knows? Even among the Aystar, there are servants and visitors from foreign lands who cannot be trusted. The Sceptre Guilds are not as tight knit as they once were, and even though the conflicts of old have ended, there are still secret societies and factions spread across the world."

Aidan shifted uncomfortably. His dreams had been disturbing, filled with dark clouds, shadows, and lightning, all converging toward him with an unsettling force. He had shared some of the details with Ahlissa before, but there was more he had yet to say. He mentioned the burning sensation on his chest that accompanied the dreams, a pain that lingered even after he awoke.

"Perhaps the lightning and shadows are tied to Kanarzand," he suggested, though he wasn't entirely sure.

Ahlissa's gaze darkened with thought. "The darkness may be related to prophecy," she mused. "But the burning sensation... that could be something more. Something far more dangerous."

She turned to face him fully, her voice lowering to a near whisper. "It may be related to the emergence of an Aethyr Mark."

Aidan blinked, taken aback by the suggestion. "Aethyr Mark? I've heard of them, but I thought they were rare; ancient magic."

"They are," Ahlissa confirmed. "Aethyr Marks are symbols of power passed down through bloodlines. They're rare and powerful, but also unpredictable. If what you've been experiencing is the early sign of an Aethyr Mark emerging, it's something to be taken very seriously."

Aidan thought back to his childhood. The memories were hazy at best, but one thing stood out. "I occasionally get an itch or a rash on my chest and shoulder," he said slowly. "I've never known why."

Ahlissa nodded thoughtfully. "And does anyone else know about your dreams?"

"Only Shaevath Tyrathalas, my spiritual mentor in the Temple of Ages, and perhaps the other Keepers of the Past," Aidan replied. He trusted Shaevath, but this revelation about the Aethyr Mark made him question if anyone could be fully trusted with this knowledge.

Ahlissa's expression grew serious. "That's why I brought you here, away from prying eyes and ears. If your mark is truly emerging, it may be an unknown one, a deviant mark."

"A deviant mark?" Aidan repeated, the term foreign yet ominous to him.

Ahlissa continued, "A deviant Aethyr Mark is one that falls outside the known marks of power. They're dangerous, uncontrollable, and feared for good reason. The last time deviant marks emerged in large numbers, it led to catastrophic wars. Many were hunted down and destroyed."

The weight of her words sank into Aidan, and a chill ran down his spine. "And what does that mean for me? Am I in danger?"

Ahlissa nodded. "Yes. But not just from the mark itself. If it is revealed that you have a deviant Aethyr Mark, you will be seen as a threat. The Sceptre Guilds might hunt you down, deeming you too dangerous to let live. They seek to control all magical power and will tolerate no rivals, especially not ones they can't predict."

Aidan clenched his fists. "But I don't even know if this mark is real. I don't feel... different. I don't feel like a threat."

"That doesn't matter," Ahlissa said, her voice sharp. "What matters is that others might perceive you as one. And that's why we need to be cautious. You must keep this hidden, Aidan. Tell no one else about the dreams or the burning sensation."

Aidan felt the weight of her words, but something else gnawed at him. "Why would my mentor, Shaevath, not have said anything if he knew? He must have sensed something..."

"Perhaps he knows, or perhaps he suspects," Ahlissa replied. "But even if he does, he may be protecting you by not revealing the truth. The Sceptre Guilds are always watching. It's possible he didn't want to put you in danger by confirming what might only be a possibility."

Aidan remained silent, his mind racing with all the implications of what she had said. His dreams, his bloodline, the danger of a deviant Aethyr Mark; it was all too much to process.

"There are those who might help you," Ahlissa said after a pause. "The

House of Tyrelis, for instance. They specialize in dealing with deviant marks. But they can't be trusted; they seek to exploit those with deviant powers for their own ends. I could arrange an audience with them, but it's a dangerous path."

"I don't want to be exploited," Aidan said firmly. "I don't want any part of that."

"I didn't think so," Ahlissa agreed. "But there are other options. The mages of Gideon City might have answers, and you've had dealings with them before. They are scholars and keepers of magical knowledge, though they are also cautious about deviants."

Aidan nodded, considering the possibility. He had made some allies in Gideon City, but he wasn't sure if they would accept him if they knew the truth about his mark; if it even existed.

"Then there are the Deathless Ones in Kharadia," Ahlissa continued. "We call them the Kale Ereshkigal, our revered ancestors. They have been present for centuries. They were alive when Aethyr Marks first appeared among the Aystar. They would know more than anyone about the deviants that emerged during that time."

Aidan sighed, the enormity of the situation settling over him like a heavy cloak.

"Deviant... that word doesn't sound good. I don't want to become something evil."

"It's possible," Ahlissa said bluntly. "And that's why there's fear around those with deviant marks. The power is unpredictable, and it can corrupt those who wield it. But not everyone succumbs to it. Some learn to control it, to use it for good. The question is whether you'll have the strength to control it if it manifests."

Aidan didn't respond right away. The idea of becoming something monstrous terrified him, but he also knew that the only way forward was to face it head-on. There was no turning back now.

"I still have my duties here with Lorian Tyraleth," Aidan said, his voice quiet. "I don't know how long this patrol will last, but after that, I might go to Gideon City."

"That sounds like a good plan," Ahlissa said, her expression softening. "When you're ready, let me know. I'll make sure you get there."

Aidan smiled faintly. "You're always so busy, though. I don't want to take up too much of your time."

Ahlissa laughed softly. "Don't worry about me. I always make time for things that matter. And besides, I have my own interests to look after as well. We'll find a way."

As they stood there, gazing out over the darkened hills, Aidan felt a strange sense of calm wash over him. The future was uncertain, and danger loomed on the horizon, but in that moment, he felt a quiet resolve. Whatever was coming, he would face it.

Ahlissa turned to her crew and gave the order to raise anchor. The Zephyr Breeze stirred to life once more, its engines humming as the ship began to move back toward Kaldorin.

"Remember, Aidan," Ahlissa said as they sailed through the night sky. "Say nothing to anyone about this. Not until we know more."

Aidan nodded, feeling the weight of her words as he prepared himself for whatever lay ahead.

When they arrived back in Kaldorin, Aidan stepped off the Zephyr Breeze and into the quiet streets of the town. He felt a strange mix of exhaustion and clarity. The conversation with Ahlissa had opened more questions than answers, but it had also given him a sense of direction.

As the airship sailed away into the night, Aidan made his way back to his quarters, ready to rest but knowing that his journey was far from over.

7

The Star Haunt

The knock came early in the morning, a soft but insistent rapping against the wooden door of Aidan's quarters. He stirred from his restless sleep and quickly rose, his body still stiff from the previous day's ride. The room was dimly lit by the first light of dawn creeping through the window, casting shadows on the sparse furnishings. As he approached the door, a familiar voice called out to him from the hallway.

"Aidan, be ready and downstairs in half an hour," Tiralas said. "The clan is assembling."

Aidan rubbed the sleep from his eyes and quickly readied himself. He pulled on his travel-worn clothes, secured his belt, and grabbed his satchel of notes and magical implements. Today, they were riding north toward a new discovery; a site revealed by the shifting sands of the desert. This was exactly the kind of work that invigorated Aidan. The ancient, forgotten, and hidden places of the world always called to him, stirring his curiosity.

After gathering his things, Aidan descended the narrow stairs of the guest house. The war clan was already abuzz with energy outside. The Kale Khestari warriors were preparing their mounts, adjusting saddles, and securing their weapons. Lorian, the warlord of the clan, stood at the front of the gathering. His presence was commanding, and as he raised his hand, the crowd quieted.

"Brave warriors and loyal brothers," Lorian began, his deep voice carrying across the assembled group. "Today, we ride north towards the Star Haunt, where a new portion of the ruined citadel has been exposed by the sands. We are tasked with making the area safe for the archaeologists who will follow. We do not expect trouble, but as you all know, the wasteland is home to all manner of creatures. Stay vigilant."

The warriors of the war clan, fierce and stoic, nodded in silent agreement. The thought of venturing into the ruins stirred something different in Aidan, though. While they prepared for combat, he was filled with anticipation for what they might find. Ruins held stories; stories etched into stone, buried in the dust of centuries.

Tiralas, his fellow warrior and newfound friend, approached him as the warriors made final preparations. "Are you ready?" he asked. "Got everything?"

Aidan patted his satchel, checking his supplies one last time. "Got everything. I'm ready."

Tiralas grinned. "Good. I hear ruins are your kind of thing. You must be excited about where we're going."

"I am," Aidan admitted. "Places like this are why I became a scholar in the first place."

"Great! Well, the last time we were there, we had to clear out an infestation of sand worms. That was messy. Lost some good men." Tiralas' expression darkened for a moment before he added with forced optimism, "But I'm sure that won't happen again."

"Let's hope not," Aidan agreed, though he couldn't shake the feeling that danger always lurked in ancient places.

With the blast of a horn, the war clan rode out, heading north across the vast arid plains. The journey was long, the sun beating down on them as they rode, but the excitement in the air kept them moving swiftly. As they rode, Aidan's mind wandered, and he found himself thinking about the name of the place they were heading to: Star Haunt.

Tiralas, sensing Aidan's curiosity, began to explain. "The Star Haunt is ancient, some say it was built in the age from before the first Khestar - the Kale Khestari - arrived in these lands. It was one of their fortresses, built to hold back the Agar tribes that once roamed this region. It fell during a siege and was lost for centuries, buried by the shifting sands. Some say it's cursed. Stories of bright lights and ghostly whispers... explorers disappearing without a trace. I've never seen anything like that myself, so I don't believe those stories."

Aidan nodded, listening intently. Curses and hauntings; these were the things of legend, and yet, he had seen enough in his life to know that such legends often had a kernel of truth.

After a full day's ride, the war clan reached the outskirts of the Star Haunt ruins. They established their encampment on the nearby sand dunes, with smaller tents serving as lookout posts to keep an eye on the desert's horizon. As night fell, the air turned cooler, and the ruins themselves stood quiet under the blanket of stars. A cluster of exposed walls and a few statues of Aystar warriors dotted the landscape, though the entrance to an underground complex was clearly visible; an ominous gateway into the depths below.

Tiralas approached Aidan again that evening. "My father tells me that a previous expedition found strange symbols on the walls inside the ruin," he said. "They couldn't read them. Not Aystar writing, but maybe arcane. Would you be able to decipher something like that?"

Aidan considered it. "Yes, I might be able to."

"Good," Tiralas said with a nod. "We'll be heading inside in the morning. Father wants to secure the perimeter first. You'll come with me to investigate the writing once it's safe."

The night passed without incident, and as dawn broke, Aidan found himself standing with Tiralas, two druids, two priests, and six warriors at the entrance to the ruins. The structure was partially buried beneath the sands, but the stairs leading down into the complex were intact. The group descended, the priests casting light spells at key points to illuminate the way.

The air inside was still, and their footsteps echoed softly through the narrow passageways. After navigating through several small, empty chambers, they arrived at a larger room. The northern wall was inscribed with a series of hieroglyphic symbols, unlike anything the priests or druids had ever seen before.

"Can you make anything out of it?" Tiralas asked as Aidan approached the wall.

The elder of the priests confirmed that the runes were magical in nature. Aidan studied them with caution and recalled his training with Shaevath, in the Temple of the Ages, where he had been taught how to call upon the Aethyr to summon a deeper understanding to identify and comprehend ancient writings or spoken tongues. But the spell alone wasn't enough to decipher the writing. Something was off. He reached for his enchanted glasses, adjusting their power to decode the arcane nature of the inscriptions.

As the runes shimmered and reformed before his eyes, Aidan saw something more. The word "unseen" leapt out at him; a command word embedded within the symbols. But there was more. The runes were layered with deception, masked by additional magic.

Realising the complexity of the enchantments, Aidan took a deep breath. He cast a new spell that would enable him to study the language again, this time while wearing the glasses. As he spoke the command word, the inscriptions shifted, transforming into a new script. This time, it was clearly Aystaran in origin.

"It's a key," Aidan said, astonished. "The writing is a key to open something; a concealed entrance. It's effectively an opening spell. I think I can open it."

The druids and priests watched in amazement as Aidan explained the nature of the spell. The warriors, meanwhile, looked nervous. They were brave, but this magic was unfamiliar and unsettling to them.

Tiralas, however, remained calm. "Do it," he said. "Let's see what lies beyond."

Aidan nodded and cast the spell. At first, nothing happened. Then, the wall began to grind and shift, sliding down into the floor with a deep, resonating groan. Beyond the wall was darkness; a long corridor that stretched out before them. Light spells flickered and dimmed as they tried to illuminate the space, and a foul stench wafted out from the newly opened passage.

Without warning, a grotesque, seething mass of rot and corruption erupted from the floor, roughly humanoid in shape but twisted beyond recognition. The creature's clawed fist lashed out, striking one of the priests and sending him sprawling to the ground.

Aidan's heart raced. The priest's body began to change, his skin paling and darkening in patches. The creature's touch was corrupting him.

"This place is cursed!" Aidan thought, panic surging through him. He could feel the malevolent energy of the creature as it advanced.

"Tiralas, the creature; it's corrupting the priest!" Aidan shouted, his voice urgent.

Tiralas, his sword drawn, was already moving to defend the group. "We fight together!" he bellowed, rallying the warriors and divine casters.

Aidan knew that they would need more than swords to defeat this creature. As he prepared to summon his magic, he could feel the oppressive weight of the Star Haunt's ancient and dark history coalesce around him.

8

The Tainted One

The creature recoiled from the torchlight like a mass of seething darkness, twisting into the shadows of the ancient cavern walls, its form boiling with malevolence. Its shape flickered between different twisted, horrific forms, as though it could not settle on one face of hatred. The room was thick with the stench of rot, and Aidan's eyes adjusted to the murky haze, enough to see that the fallen priest was still alive, albeit horrifically altered. His skin was marred with sickly lesions, peeling away like papery strips, as if burned from the inside by a dark, corrupting force. The sight filled Aidan with a cold certainty; this was the effect of taint.

The priests, horrified yet resolute, began chanting to the ancestral spirits, their voices shaky but determined to maintain some protection against the creature's penetrating malice. Tiralas, a seasoned warrior and their commander, quickly signalled his warriors to form a defensive line, their scimitars raised in tight formation, shields locked to create an impassable barrier between the fiend and their vulnerable priests. Meanwhile, one of the priests dragged his afflicted companion to safety, pouring a sacred remedy over the wounds in an attempt to halt the dark corruption spreading through him.

Aidan approached the priest administering the healing ritual. "What's happening to him?" he asked, noting the extent of the disfigurement overtaking the man.

"He's afflicted," the priest replied, keeping his hands steady despite the fear in his voice. "These lesions... they're unnatural. I fear they are a physical manifestation of pure darkness."

Aidan studied the fallen priest, nodding solemnly. "He's been tainted by that creature. I've seen it before."

A sudden hiss echoed from the shadows. One of the warriors tensed, his gaze locked on the creature as it began to unfurl itself. "It moves again..."

"Hold the line!" Tiralas ordered, his voice steady, yet Aidan could sense the underlying dread. "We cannot let it pass."

"It is bound here," the elder priest muttered as though reminding himself. "A guardian of great evil. This corruption has twisted its purpose."

Drawing his enchanted bow, Aidan readied an arrow. "Priests, do what you can. If there's a potent blessing or ward left among you, use it now; our only chance is to weaken it while it's still restrained."

As Aidan prepared his shot, the creature loomed at the entrance, as if testing their resolve. Its unrestrained rage poured out like icy tendrils that clawed at each of them, seeping into their souls and chilling them to the bone.

"Is it undead?" Tiralas asked, his voice barely a whisper.

The elder priest shook his head, his eyes wide with helplessness. "Its nature is elusive... undead, perhaps, but something else also lingers. A defilement beyond death. It mocks our prayers as though they are meaningless chants."

The warriors gripped their scimitars more tightly. Then, with sickening speed, two massive, clawed arms shot out from the darkness, slamming against the line of warriors with unnatural force. They were thrown like rag dolls, shields clattering as they struggled back into formation, visibly shaken but unwavering.

In response, Tiralas shouted an incantation, and from his hand streamed small glowing projectiles, aimed directly at the creature. They hit, but the beast absorbed the strikes as though they were mere annoyances. Its rage only deepened, and a low, rumbling laugh vibrated through the chamber, as though it revelled in their resistance.

Aidan released an arrow, striking the creature dead-on. The arrow sank in but did little to halt the monstrosity, which seemed to reshape itself and retreat slightly, only to bellow out in a language unfamiliar to most, yet chillingly resonant.

The priests recoiled, retreating further. The warriors formed a tighter line around them as Aidan felt the words crawl into his mind, unbidden, comprehensible through some twisted, dark affinity he'd picked up in his dealings with forbidden knowledge.

"Who disturbs my slumber... who breaks the seal..." The words seethed with contempt, and the creature's tone dripped with venom.

Aidan steadied himself, projecting his voice back into the depths. "We come seeking knowledge. If you are a threat to this land, then we will see you destroyed."

"You dare?" The creature's voice dripped with malevolence. "Only my masters hold dominion here. You, mortal... you are nothing."

Tiralas looked over, alarmed, as Aidan's strange understanding of the creature's tongue dawned on him. "You can understand it?"

Aidan nodded grimly. "Yes."

Tiralas's gaze was laced with fear. "Then beware. This entity is here to guard something sacred to its own vile kind."

Ignoring the commander's warning, Aidan stepped closer. "Tell me, creature, who are your masters?"

"Those who came before you... those whose power predates your kind," it sneered.

The priests chanted louder, their voices trembling as they backed further into the corridor. The warriors cast nervous glances, sensing the weight of a power beyond their understanding pressing down on them.

"Show yourself fully," Aidan demanded, stepping forward.

A snarl echoed from the darkness, followed by a guttural, mocking laugh. "You dare to command me?" Slowly, it slithered forward, morphing, expanding into a massive, hideous form; a writhing, corrupt mass that towered above him, festering with hatred. A blast of putrid stench filled the corridor, enough to make some of the warriors retch where they stood. The creature's cold, soulless eyes locked on Aidan, sizing him up with a malignant intensity. "You're no warrior. You're barely mortal... you reek of taint. I could devour you, half-blood, and feed my hunger."

"Then do it," Aidan challenged, forcing his voice to remain steady. "If I'm so weak, why don't you?"

The creature's laughter erupted again, its voice curling through the darkness like poisoned smoke. "Come closer then, half-blood, and know your worthlessness."

Aidan took a step forward, ignoring the shouts from Tiralas behind him. "If your masters feared this place would be found, they should have marked it better. Now it lies open."

The guardian sneered, its eyes narrowing with contempt. "You will die slowly... but your spirit will be mine."

It lunged, and Aidan had only a moment to brace before it struck, sending him sprawling back with crushing force. White-hot pain shot through his chest, and he felt the dark taint gnawing at his senses, twisting and corrupting him. He gasped as the burning sensation pulsed within him, more searing than his worst nightmares.

A sickening realization settled over him as the creature's voice resonated within his mind. "This cannot be... your blood... it's marked with my master's signature..."

Aidan forced himself to his feet, weakened but defiant. "If my blood is theirs, then your threats mean nothing."

The creature hissed, seething with loathing. "Then give me your spirit, half-blood. Submit... or face endless agony."

Aidan gritted his teeth. "No. If I am of your master's kind, then prove your worth; allow me through."

The beast hesitated, wavering as if bound by some ancient rule. "You defy my hunger, yet you are kin... very well. Enter, if you dare. But only you... your blood alone grants you access."

The creature morphed, retreating into the darkness as it revealed a winding passage beyond. "Go now, mortal... or your strength will fail you soon enough."

Aidan felt his knees trembling but took a step forward, ignoring the anguish clawing at his heart. He moved past the writhing beast, alone, descending down a dark stairway into the deeper unknown. The darkness grew thicker, almost palpable, pressing in around him like a suffocating force. The taint pulsed in his veins, resonating with a strange energy that seemed to connect him to the creature's vile essence.

After a winding descent, he found himself before a sealed, black door. Its surface bore an intricate, serpentine symbol that glowed faintly under his enchanted glasses. With a steadying breath, he traced the markings and pushed the door open, revealing a dimly lit chamber.

Inside, a long, stone table stretched before him, flanked by empty chairs, yet his vision flickered as if seeing through time itself. Fourteen dark, cold figures appeared around the table, speaking in low, harsh tones. A council of war. These beings were not Aystar, yet they felt linked to him in some forgotten way.

They discussed the city's defences, their pale faces set in grim determination, and Aidan's heart pounded as he took in their alien presence. They were an ancient people; powerful, merciless, and cold. These were no ordinary beings, nor were they the tainted souls he had encountered before. They were something beyond; forebears from an older, darker age.

As he stood there, he sensed a word forming in his mind, unbidden but undeniable: *Kale Ashtari*. With a shiver, he realised he was not alone in this room nor fully himself. He was a link in a chain of dark bloodlines stretching back through countless ages. The vision faded, and he found himself alone once more, haunted by what he had seen; a fleeting glimpse into the past.

He regained his composure and stepped inside.

9

The Corrupted Tongue

Upon entering the chamber, Aidan surveyed his surroundings, noting the three doors that opened onto different parts of the fortress. The atmosphere within the vast, shadowy hall felt heavy with secrets, as though centuries of lives, ambitions, and tragedies lingered in the air. Each door hinted at different paths and choices, paths that had once served a thriving community, now left empty but for faint echoes and memories hidden beneath the dust.

The eastern door led to the ablutions, living quarters, and sleeping areas; spaces that had once been filled with daily routines and private moments. A faint sense of rest and peace lingered in those rooms, the last traces of lives once lived, now stilled. The northern door, however, drew him to the practical heart of the fortress: kitchens, storerooms, and a communal dining room that had once bustled with laughter and the clink of eating utensils. Here, the remnants of sustenance hinted at the community's need for survival and nourishment, simple and vital.

It was the western door, however, that pulled him most strongly. Through it lay the fortress's arsenal: armouries, training rooms, chambers for magical research, and, crucially, a small but invaluable library. The pull was almost physical, urging him towards it with an intensity he could not ignore. Aidan felt certain this door led to knowledge that might illuminate mysteries not yet fully revealed.

As he stepped through, a sense of weight bore down upon him, the kind of pressure felt when one stood in places steeped in history. It was as though the knowledge within this small library itself pressed on him, whispering promises of answers to questions he had not yet dared to ask. Though modest in size, the library's contents felt curated, with each text and scroll preserved, not by chance but by deliberate care.

Once inside, Aidan's gaze drifted over the rows of shelves, filled with fragile scrolls and ancient tomes, some crumbling with age, others preserved by the fading remnants of magical wards. The preservation spells, though weakened, held strong enough to shield the most valuable texts from decay, safeguarding a knowledge that was far too dangerous to fade. What truly captivated him, however, was the focus of the knowledge in this library. These were not mere histories or treatises on magic. Rather, they were precise and intentional records, dedicated to one theme alone: the Kale Ashtari, an ancient, enigmatic race, and their dealings with forces both mortal and divine.

Aidan traced his fingers over a set of scrolls that seemed to pulse with latent power. Each one detailed ancient Kale Ashtari lore, from their esoteric rites to accounts of a primordial era known as the Age of Darkness. His pulse quickened as he recognised mention of the "marks of power," early manifestations of what were now known as Aethyr Marks. These texts implied that long before the term "Aethyr Marks" was coined, the Kale Ashtari had borne similar marks, powers bound into their very essence by a force beyond understanding.

As he read, a startling thought struck him: Could it be that the Kale Ashtari were the first to bear these marks, generations before his own people? The implications shook Aidan. If these were the origins of the marks, then much of what he had believed about his heritage was suddenly called into question. Had his people's most sacred knowledge been but a shadow of the ancient lore preserved here? He felt a strange resonance as he traced the symbols with his fingers, the same symbols he had once studied on a different path, far from here.

According to the fortress's records, the stronghold had once served as a sanctuary, a bastion of power for one of the most feared and powerful Kale Ashtari clans. This clan, surrounded by unimaginable horrors, had made a fateful choice: they would fight fire with fire. Their creed became one of power through mastery over darkness, a dark yet calculated resolve to turn their enemies' own corrupting force against them. They believed that in doing so, they could become impenetrable, unbreakable, defending their sanctuary with a level of power so profound that no mortal or immortal threat could breach it.

With each scroll, Aidan felt the dark weight of this knowledge bearing down on him, as though centuries of resolve and depravity imprinted themselves into his bones. Strangely, as the hours passed, he noticed the persistent pain in his chest - a sensation that had troubled him for days - had begun to fade, almost as if the knowledge he consumed soothed him, filling a void that had long been left untended. The longer he read, the more he felt the pain dissolving, as though his body was finally aligning with some hidden truth he'd been evading.

Lost in the scrolls, he scribbled notes in his personal journal, filling page after page with coded shorthand, knowing that the contents of these texts must remain secure. This knowledge, dangerous as it was,

was his alone, at least for now.

Eventually, Aidan tore himself away from the shelves and took a final look at the texts, sensing a profound transformation within himself. He had glimpsed the darkest depths of Kale Ashtari lore, and in doing so, had awakened parts of himself he scarcely understood. He rose, his body feeling both lightened and laden, and began to make his way back through the labyrinthine corridors, reluctantly leaving behind the vault of knowledge he could scarcely believe he had just encountered.

As he approached the guardian's corridor, the creature still loomed in the darkness, a silent sentinel watching the threshold. As Aidan neared, it shifted slightly, granting him passage without the hostility it had initially shown. Its voice, a deep, menacing growl, filled the narrow corridor.

"Did you find what you were looking for?" the guardian asked, its tone a mix of curiosity and veiled menace.

"Yes," Aidan replied, his voice steady. "I saw their vision, their plans, and I understand their purpose now. I see my connection to them, and I see why you were set here to guard this place."

The guardian regarded him for a long moment. "Then you understand that this sanctuary is not lost. One day, it may rise again, restored. When that day comes, you will be welcome. When you leave, I will seal the way. But know this; you can return if you choose."

Aidan nodded. "I do understand. And when I am ready, I may return, once I have fully uncovered the story of those who built this sanctuary."

The guardian inclined its head, acknowledging Aidan's resolve. "You have seen the truth and survived it. Now go."

As Aidan moved to leave, a question formed in his mind, compelling him to turn back. "Could the words on the entrance be changed? To prevent others from entering?"

The guardian chuckled darkly, the sound reverberating through the passage. "Not by my hand. I guard this place. And any who attempt entry, I will destroy; as I could have destroyed you."

"Yes," Aidan said thoughtfully, "you could have."

"But your essence resonated true, and thus I permitted your passage."

The guardian stepped aside, and Aidan crossed the threshold, the chamber echoing with the finality of the door sealing itself behind him. Following the winding corridors, he emerged at last into the cold light of the surface.

The warriors of his war clan awaited him, their faces etched with relief and wariness alike. His time below had altered him, and he bore the signs of one who had walked amidst things both dreadful and sacred. Tiralas, his commander, was among them, and he waved the other warriors back as he stepped forward, his gaze locked on Aidan.

"I have brought healers," Tiralas said, signalling a group of priests forward. "They have salves to restore your strength."

The priests approached, chanting softly as they applied the restorative balms to Aidan's wounds. The fatigue that clung to him began to lift, yet he sensed the air around him grow thick with tension as his comrades exchanged uneasy glances.

"Your time with that guardian and in those ancient halls has changed you," Tiralas said quietly. "The others have grown... concerned. It is said that you spoke a dark tongue within the walls."

Aidan inclined his head. "I understand their concern. Perhaps it is best if I return to Kharadia, to resume my studies."

Tiralas nodded approvingly. "You have served well. You can leave knowing that there is no dishonour in it." His voice softened. "We will summon transport for you, to take you where you must go."

Aidan felt a pang of regret but understood the wisdom in Tiralas's suggestion. Together, they set off across the harsh desert landscape, the sun casting long shadows across the sands as they trekked toward a small oasis. There, they waited in silence for the Zephyr Breeze to arrive, both knowing it would soon carry Aidan away from the fortress's secrets but closer to truths he could not yet fathom.

Tiralas handed Aidan a flask of water and met his gaze with a look that carried both respect and unspoken warning.

"You've walked the path of darkness, Aidan," Tiralas murmured. "But remember, you also carry the strength to resist it. Take care, brother."

Aidan offered a solemn nod in response.

Tiralas's tone softens slightly as he adds, "Despite your... oddness, I trust you. You might have noticed I dabble in the magical arts myself."

With that, Tiralas turns and begins his trek back across the sand dunes, leaving Aidan alone at the oasis.

10

The Oasis

Aidan sat beside the tranquil pool of water, surrounded by scattered rocks and sparse patches of greenery. The oasis offered a rare moment of stillness, far removed from the chaos of the sanctuary he had just left behind. The wind was soft, carrying with it the faint scent of the desert. He took a deep breath, savouring the peace.

This was no ordinary oasis. To a casual observer, it was simply a pleasant reprieve from the relentless heat of the plains and dunes. But to Aidan, it was a place of reflection, where he could begin to unravel the mysteries that had consumed his mind since leaving the ancient Kale Ashtari fortress.

He scanned his surroundings, alert for any signs that he might be watched. The warriors from his patrol had left him here on orders, but his instincts never fully relaxed. After everything he had witnessed and learned, vigilance had become second nature.

His eyes narrowed as they swept over the horizon, but nothing was out of place. No movement in the shadows. No hidden threats. Aidan exhaled slowly, satisfied that he was alone, at least for now.

An hour passed in contemplative silence before a shadow crossed the sky. The Zephyr Breeze, an elegant airship, appeared from the horizon, gliding smoothly over the dunes. Aidan watched as it descended gracefully on the far side of the oasis. Its polished hull gleamed in the sunlight as it hovered just above the ground, a gangplank extending from its side.

Aidan rose to his feet, his thoughts already turning to the events that awaited him beyond this quiet refuge. He climbed aboard, greeted by members of Ahlissa's crew, who escorted him directly to the bridge. The warmth of the crew's welcome brought a sense of relief after his encounter with the Kale Ashtari guardian, and he thanked them graciously.

Ahlissa herself greeted him with a warm embrace, her eyes twinkling with the kind of amusement only an old friend could muster. "You look like you've been through a lot," she said, eyeing him with concern. "Come, let's get you something to drink."

She signalled to one of her assistants, who returned shortly with a cool drink. Ahlissa instructed the airship to continue to its destination and beckoned Aidan to follow her to the rear-facing observation deck. There, they settled into plush leather recliners, surrounded by food and drink within easy reach.

Ahlissa's demeanour shifted, her tone becoming more serious as she inquired, "So, how are you, Aidan? I must admit, this urgent call to retrieve you from your patrol was quite the surprise."

"It surprised me, too," Aidan admitted.

"So, what happened? What have you done wrong?" she asked with a raised eyebrow, her curiosity piqued.

Aidan sighed and began recounting the events. "We entered an ancient sanctuary, and within, we found a sealed door. I opened it, revealing a corrupted, tainted guardian that immediately attacked us. It was a creature of pure malice, but I was able to communicate with it; using a dark language. That's when my Aethyr Mark began reacting, stronger than it ever had before. The guardian sensed it, recognised it, and allowed me to pass. It saw me as part of its own kind, or at least connected to its masters. Beyond that door, I found a room... and a vision."

Ahlissa listened intently as Aidan described the figures he had seen, their ancient, cold malice, and the powerful threats they had discussed; monstrous beings, shadow creatures and entities from The Eternal Void. Aidan could still feel the weight of their words, the depth of their history. "At first, I thought they were Aystar," he continued, "but these beings were older... much older. Their race predates anything I've ever encountered. They are the Kale Ashtari. They spoke of using corruption as a weapon against their enemies, and yet I didn't sense that all of them were inherently evil. What's more, the texts in their library revealed something astonishing: they may have been the first to bear the marks of power, long before we called them Aethyr Marks."

He paused, watching as Ahlissa's expression shifted to one of deep contemplation. "They weren't of this world, Ahlissa. They were here during the Age of Darkness, and they left this world when their sanctuary was abandoned. But before they did, they seeded their bloodline into a lesser race on Kharadia, intending to fulfil a prophecy in a later age."

Ahlissa took in the weight of his words. "And the guardian...?"

"The guardian is the manifestation of their corruption," Aidan said, his voice softening. "It told me I would be welcome back anytime. But anyone else who tries to enter would be killed. My only crime, in the eyes of my war band, was speaking in the dark tongue. They were glad to be rid of me."

Ahlissa nodded, her face serious as she processed everything he had shared. "My, my... you've become quite the adventurer," she said after a moment. "Look at you; out there facing tainted guardians and unravelling ancient prophecies. That's more excitement than you've seen in quite a while, stuck with all your fascinating books."

Aidan chuckled. "Oh, they suggested I return to my books. But I've read what I can. I'm not sure where to go next."

Ahlissa leaned back in her chair, eyes gazing out at the dunes below. "So, where do you think you'll head? Scylla is a big place. Right now, I'm headed for Gideon City, but after that... who knows?"

"The 'who knows' part sounds intriguing," Aidan replied with a smile.

"It could be," she said, her grin mischievous. "Depends on what the next contract is."

"Gideon seems like the logical choice for me," Aidan mused. "I might be able to get this taint removed there. But then again... what if my mark is tied to the taint? I really don't know."

Ahlissa's brow furrowed slightly. "If it's advice or healing you're after, the temples in Gideon City might be a good place to start."

"The problem is, who can I even talk to about this Aethyr Mark? It's not exactly something I can casually discuss with just anyone."

Ahlissa nodded thoughtfully. "True. But in the big city, there are all kinds of people; and factions. I've heard rumours that The Seeker and The Sentinel have been recruiting people to search for unregistered Aethyr Marks. A small group, very low-profile, but they're active in Gideon. Sent by the Sceptre Guilds, if rumours are to be believed."

Aidan's mind raced at the possibilities. If this group was actively searching for people like him, it could be an opportunity; or a danger. "And if I want healing?" he asked.

"The Monks at the Temple of Twilight Calm don't ask many questions," Ahlissa explained. "They offer healing in exchange for services or donations. It's up to you how you repay them; if they can remove your taint. That is, if you even want it gone."

Aidan considered her words. "I'm still not sure. There's so much I don't understand about this mark..."

Ahlissa smiled sympathetically. "If you want, you can stick around with me for a while. Work with the crew, pay your way, and figure out what you want to do."

Aidan returned her smile. "I think I'd like that. It's been a long time since I've felt like I belonged anywhere."

"Good," Ahlissa said warmly. "You're welcome to have a room on board, or you can find lodgings when we dock. But if you're staying with me, I'd like to strike a deal."

Aidan raised an eyebrow, intrigued. "What sort of deal?"

"You stay aboard in exchange for lodgings and food. And if we come across anything interesting during our travels - artifacts, magical items, or the like - you help us examine them. Do the necessary research. You know how much I like to operate under the radar, so any knowledge you gain stays between us. Some of my work... let's just say it isn't always above board. We have an understanding?"

Aidan nodded. "Yes, we do."

"Good. There's one more thing," Ahlissa added, her tone playful. "You'll need to dress like one of my crew. Blend in. Is that all right with you?"

Aidan grinned. "Of course, though I feel like I should earn that first."

"What did you have in mind?" she asked, amused.

"Well, I've travelled with you before, spent time with the crew. I think I'm already part of the team, don't you?"

Ahlissa laughed. "Fair enough. The crew already likes you, and some of them are half-Aystar like you, so there's no prejudice here. Your mark - if that's what it is - hasn't fully manifested yet, so we can keep things quiet. No one on board knows what you've told me, and it will stay that way. You're safe."

Aidan felt a warmth he hadn't experienced in a long time. "Thank you. It's good to be among friends again."

"It's settled then; welcome aboard," Ahlissa said, her smile bright. "Now, what do you say we head down town and enjoy a fine dinner?"

As the Zephyr Breeze glided smoothly into Gideon's dock, Aidan felt a sense of anticipation. A new chapter of his life was beginning, and though the path ahead was uncertain, he knew that whatever lay beyond the horizon, he would face it with determination and strength.

The airship connected with the dock, and the crew began their preparations to disembark. Aidan stood at the railing, looking out over the sprawling city of Gideon, ready for whatever awaited him next.

11

One Night in Gideon

Aidan was escorted to his private quarters on the second deck of the Zephyr Breeze by one of the crew members, a half-Aystar woman named Tanith. She greeted him warmly, "Your quarters are ready. You'll find suitable attire and private facilities inside, so you can clean up before heading out tonight. Have a pleasant evening in the city." She smiled. "It's good to have you back on board. Ahlissa speaks fondly of you."

Aidan smiled and thanked her before entering the room. His quarters were modest but comfortable, consisting of two rooms: a bedroom with a set of drawers, a footlocker, and a wardrobe, as well as a smaller bathroom area with a shower and toilet. The lighting was controlled not by magic, as was common, but through a small touch panel on the wall. Aidan mused at the technology.

"Khestar technology?" he thought, recalling the lightning towers and steam engines of Kanarzand that once powered the frontier town with a form of energy the mages called "electricity." The ship's lighting system seemed similar; self-contained and independent. "This ship is something special," he thought. "But then again, it's the only one I've been on. Maybe they're all like this."

After thoroughly washing - his first real clean in weeks - Aidan felt refreshed. In the wardrobe, he found a variety of clothing, but the most appealing outfit was a set of dark green leather trousers, a fine black silk shirt, a gold and silver embroidered waistcoat, and soft-soled calf-length boots. He noticed a selection of flowing robes and accessories - neck chains, brooches, headbands, belts, and bracelets - but stuck with the simpler ensemble. The clothes fit him perfectly, almost as if tailored for him.

After making sure his personal equipment was safely stored in the footlocker, which was locked by a magical key, Aidan left his quarters to find Ahlissa.

He found her on the observation deck. It was a calm, warm night, and Ahlissa was resplendent in a flowing blue and white dress that hugged her figure elegantly. She wore a delicate gold headband with a garnet set into it, a long platinum chain adorned with an amethyst and diamond-studded amulet, and silver-coloured high-heeled shoes; quite the change from her usual boots. She smiled warmly as Aidan approached.

"You look stunning," Aidan remarked, blushing slightly at his own boldness.

Ahlissa's smile widened, clearly pleased. "I see you've recovered from your desert exploits and dressed for the occasion," she teased. "You've chosen well." Aidan sensed she approved of his outfit, putting him more at ease. "We're going to the Liberty Spire tonight for dinner and dancing," she told him. "I think you'll enjoy it."

Aidan knew the Liberty Spire was a place frequented by the elite and wealthy of Gideon. It was not the kind of place someone of his standing would typically visit, especially given Ahlissa's reputation as a roguish airship captain. He found it surprising that she would go to such an exclusive location.

Ahlissa seemed to read his thoughts and laughed. "Don't worry, you'll be fine. We're welcome there. My business dealings afford me certain luxuries, and I work for some... interesting clients."

Aidan smiled nervously. "I just hope I don't make a fool of myself on the dance floor."

"After a few drinks, I'm sure you'll be fine," she replied with a wink.

They descended from the airship docking station and walked down a long flight of stairs into the Commerce Quarter. Even at night, the city's bustling trade continued, with street vendors and shops still open. As they walked, Aidan's thoughts drifted back to his time on the streets before he had been discovered by the mages and brought into their world of arcane knowledge. Everything seemed busier now, more alive. He realised how isolated he had been with his books for so long.

"Penny for your thoughts?" Ahlissa teased, noticing his distraction.

"Just remembering my life on the streets before the mages found me," Aidan replied with a small smile. "It's a different world from being a bookworm these last few years."

Ahlissa nodded. "I imagine so."

They crossed through the Commerce Quarter, where Ahlissa hailed an air barge to take them across the floating rock islands and between towers to the Pleasure Quarter. There, they disembarked onto a wide platform that spanned a massive gap between two towers, leading to the entrance of the Liberty Spire.

Two attendants dressed in black trousers, white shirts, crimson over-coats, and gold-trimmed top hats greeted them warmly. "Good evening, Lady Ahlissa," one of them said with a gracious smile. "Your table for two is ready and waiting inside. Is there anything you or your companion may require?"

"No, thank you, Anders. We're fine this evening," Ahlissa replied, returning his smile before leading Aidan inside.

They walked along a red carpet through an ornately decorated hall, eventually entering a lavish ballroom and banquet hall. Aidan marvelled at the large dance floor, live band, and the sumptuous spread laid out on long tables. A bar and side kitchen served the guests, while a door leading to another entertainment area bore the sign "Casino."

Surveying the room, Aidan noted several high-ranking bureaucrats and officials, along with a few faces that seemed familiar from his time in Kanarzand. He caught a glimpse of an older man with glasses; possibly his former mentor, Master Brevax. Across the room, an alluring young woman with dark hair and heavy makeup seemed to be staring at him, dressed in red and silver with matching shoes.

Ahlissa leaned over and whispered, "See that group over there? The

Aystaran Ambassador and his retinue. Five are Aystar from Kharadia, but that hooded figure is... different. Not eating or drinking. I suspect it might be a deathless envoy from Kale Ereshkigal."

Aidan nodded, intrigued.

An attendant escorted them to a private table for two near the corner, offering a clear view of the ballroom. After placing their order, the waiter informed them that drinks would arrive soon, and dinner would follow within half an hour. "Everything has already been paid for, as always," he added with a smile.

Ahlissa thanked him and turned her attention to Aidan. "So, what are you thinking? I imagine this isn't your usual scene."

"I'm just surprised by how well you're known here," Aidan admitted. "Given your natural beauty, though, I imagine walking in company like this is nothing new for you."

Ahlissa laughed softly. "Let's just say my business clients make sure I'm well-treated. I know things. They know I know things. It's all part of the arrangement. This place is perfect for keeping in touch and finding new clients... plus, I enjoy the food and entertainment."

Aidan hesitated before asking, "But wouldn't people wonder who I am? Why someone like me is here with you?"

Ahlissa waved his concern away. "Not at all. You're a fine young man here for a delightful evening. No one will question it."

He mentioned the young woman who had been staring at him earlier.

Ahlissa raised an eyebrow, her lips curling into a teasing smile. "Perhaps I'm not the only woman who finds you intriguing. Sounds like I have some competition," she quipped.

Soon, wine arrived at their table; an excellent vintage, by Aidan's judgment. Ahlissa consumed several glasses, encouraging him to do the same. He was cautious not to overindulge, wanting to stay in control. After a couple of drinks, though, he felt a pleasant buzz and relaxed more, enjoying the atmosphere and Ahlissa's company.

The excitement of the evening invigorated Aidan, and he found himself able to unwind, feeling lighter and more at ease.

The food, when it arrived, was exquisite; a variety of meats and dishes seasoned with exotic spices. He and Ahlissa made small talk, discussing her travels and his recent experiences.

"Time to dance!" Ahlissa exclaimed suddenly, pulling him to the dance floor.

Aidan followed her lead, though he was unsure of the steps. Despite his lack of experience, he managed to keep up, finding his rhythm as the music swirled around them. The dance floor itself was a marvel, slowly rising above the main floor and suspending them in mid-air as the band played enchanting, orchestral pieces followed by more energetic, rhythmic tunes.

As they danced, Aidan once again noticed the woman in red from earlier. She was still watching him, her gaze lingering for a moment before she smiled and turned away, no longer acknowledging him for the rest of the evening.

The dance ended, and as the guests returned to their tables for more food and conversation, Ahlissa excused herself to visit the ladies' room. Aidan stood politely as she left, then sat back down. The waiter returned briefly to refill their wine, offering another warm smile.

"Is everything to your satisfaction, young master?" the waiter asked.

"Yes, everything is wonderful. Thank you," Aidan replied.

After the waiter left, Aidan noticed someone waving to him from a nearby table. To his surprise, it was Master Brevax. The older man approached and took Ahlissa's seat in her absence.

"Aidan, my boy! It's been so long!" Master Brevax exclaimed. "I feared something terrible had happened to you after Kanarzand fell. What became of you?"

Aidan briefly recounted the last moments of his time in Kanarzand; the attack, the chaos, the fleeing with the Wasteland Druid.

Master Brevax nodded solemnly. "A difficult time for us all. And now? What are you doing these days? I hope someone has noticed your skill with libraries. Have you found a place here?"

"Actually, I've been travelling with Ahlissa and her crew," Aidan explained. "It's been... enlightening."

Master Brevax's eyes lit up. "Ah, yes. The famous captain. You've found quite an adventurous companion! I'm stationed here at the Cordovar Academic Centre. It's a prestigious institution, sponsored by the Cordovar Library. Exciting work for me; lots of research for the

Seeker and the Gatherer. Still, I miss Kanarzand... Those were good days before the evil came."

Aidan leans forward and quietly asks "Whatever came of Lord Khannay?"

Master Brevax again looks serious. "He was murdered. A team of outsiders attacked him in his private quarters when they broke into his tower. Nothing remained of him except an ash stain on his fancy carpets. The rumours doing the rounds imply that Lord Khannay was a vampire with connections to some kind of cult. It was a tragic circumstance, and his killers were never brought to justice as they fled the scene. The implication that he was a vampire was never proven and I was certainly unaware if that was ever true."

There was a sadness in Brevax's voice as he continued. "I must admit, I was shocked by your discoveries beneath the library. A sentient space? Unbelievable; until you described it. I'd love to hear more of your experiences."

"I'd be happy to write them down for you," Aidan offered. "My notes are extensive, and I could make an exclusive copy for the Cordovar Academic Centre."

Master Brevax's face brightened. "That would be magnificent! It would be an honour to include your account in our collection. Few have recognised the significance of what you witnessed."

"Send me a blank tome and writing supplies to the Zephyr Breeze," Aidan suggested. "I'll begin as soon as I can."

"That can be arranged," Brevax said. "Oh, and I'll include a spell that can transcribe notes automatically. Surprised you don't already know it, Aidan."

Aidan chuckled. "I've been a little out of practice."

Master Brevax grew more serious. "I'm planning an expedition back to Kanarzand someday, to salvage what remains of our old museum and library. When the time comes, would you join me?"

"Absolutely," Aidan replied. "Perhaps Ahlissa could help with the transport."

Master Brevax smiled at the idea. "That's good news. I'll let you know when the preparations begin."

Before Brevax could say more, Ahlissa returned to the table. She gave Master Brevax a polite smile as she approached.

"Lady Ahlissa," Brevax said, bowing slightly. "It's a pleasure to see you again."

"And you, Master Brevax," she replied. "I hope young Aidan hasn't been too overwhelmed by your scholarly talk."

"Not at all, my lady," Brevax chuckled. "Though I must be going. Good fortune to you both in your travels."

As Brevax returned to his table, Ahlissa watched him closely.

"I am being cautious, Aidan, that is all." Ahlissa says rather curtly. "Old friends and acquaintances may not necessarily be who they claim or seem. We have all experienced some dark times and this is now a time of renewal. But we must never forget that old alliances and indeed ancient powers still lie in wait across this land. Gideon City is a melting pot of espionage, and every group has planted agents everywhere. Who did Master Brevax tell you that he is now working for?"

"He is working for the Cordovar Academic Centre." Aidan says. "He is looking at returning to Kanarzand in the future to find what remains of the library. If there is anything to be perhaps suspicious of, two things come to mind. Firstly, he noticed there was a change in me, which you heard and secondly, he may have been under the influence at some time, of Lord Khannay, who I learned was a vampire and is now dead. I was careful to ensure that he knew nothing of what has happened recently."

Ahlissa appears to visibly relax and then she says "The very same Lord Khannay who was exposed as a vampire with links back to the enclave of cultists near the border of Sindarr? Now I am not suggesting that Master Brevax knew of Khannay's affiliations or true nature but quite unwittingly he did serve such an influential master. It could be again that he is working for people who might use his good nature to learn more about you. You must be careful, I am very concerned for you. I hear what you are telling me, so that does allay some concerns. Do you wish for me to have his new role at the Cordovar Academic Centre investigated?"

"Yes, if you would not mind ... I respect Master Brevax, and I would not like him to be used as the pawn in someone else's game."

"I understand. My friends will be discreet in their investigation. Anything untoward will be revealed to us but will not be acted upon unless you tell us it is OK."

"Perhaps you might want to find out, if you can, if his plan to go back to Kanarzand is his ... or is he being manipulated or directed by another influence to do so. If that is the case, then there must be something there that needs to be recovered."

"That could be true, but rest assured we will learn what lies at the heart of that matter. Come now, why are we being so serious ... let us continue enjoying the atmosphere and finish our meal."

They dined and conversed late into the evening, eventually retreating to their room upstairs to rest.

12

An Unusual Contact

Ahlissa and Aidan entered the luxurious lobby of the Liberty Spire, its grandeur apparent in every corner, from the polished marble floors to the magically lit chandeliers that hung like delicate stars. The air was filled with the subtle hum of magic, and in front of them, elevators stood ready. These weren't ordinary elevators; they were arcane lifts, designed to transport guests through the tower with speed and elegance. One of the attendants waved them in, and they ascended to the 26th floor in a blur of motion.

When the doors opened, they were greeted by a magnificent suite. Aidan was immediately struck by the room's grandeur. Its centrepiece was a wide balcony that overlooked the sprawling city, the lights of the city sparkling like jewels on a velvet cloth. Beyond the city, Aidan could see the expansive desert stretching out, the horizon blending into the sky. The sight was breathtaking, a stark reminder of how far he had come from the streets and libraries of lower Gideon City.

Ahlissa, noticing his awe, smiled as she prepared herself for bed. "Rest, Aidan," she said softly, her voice soothing after the excitement of the night. "We'll be travelling north tomorrow. I have a consignment to deliver, and we need to be on our way within four days."

Aidan nodded, still taking in the beauty of the view. As he returned to the room, a thought crossed his mind; Where am I supposed to rest? The room had only one large bed, which Ahlissa was already making herself comfortable in. Sensing his hesitation, Ahlissa turned to him with a soft laugh.

"You look uncomfortable; what's the matter? There's only one bed in this room, but don't worry," she said, her eyes twinkling with amusement. "We can share it. I won't bite."

Aidan blushed, unsure of how to respond. After a moment's pause, he reluctantly climbed into the bed but stayed on the far edge, keeping a respectful distance. As he settled in, Ahlissa reached over and touched his shoulder affectionately, her voice gentle. "Sleep well, Aidan. This has been a beautiful night with beautiful company."

Aidan smiled. "It has," he admitted softly, still flustered by her presence so close.

"Good," she said, her tone more serious now. "Rest. You need to keep your wits about you, especially with the tasks we have ahead. My crew will say nothing of our time together, if that's what you're worried about. And you'll want to get rid of any potential hangover by the morning." She smiled once more before turning away to sleep.

With that, they both drifted off into a peaceful slumber, the quiet hum of the city below lulling them into rest.

The next morning, sunlight streamed through the balcony doors, casting a warm glow across the room. They both rose and dressed, ready for the day ahead. Breakfast was brought to their room; an impressive spread of cereals, fruits, and a variety of hot dishes, including spiced meats and eggs. They decided to eat on the balcony, enjoying the fresh air and the view of the waking city.

As they ate, Ahlissa looked over at Aidan. "Did you enjoy the evening we shared here last night?" she asked, a hint of teasing in her voice.

"Yes, indeed," Aidan said, though there was a slight hesitation in his voice. He paused for a moment, glancing at Ahlissa before continuing. "Look, I think you know how I feel about you... so I was thinking last night, why me?"

Ahlissa paused mid-bite and set her fork down. She looked at Aidan, her gaze steady and thoughtful. "Because you're here, Aidan. You're travelling with me, and you're available. You needed to relax and reacquaint yourself with a large city. Granted, this isn't the typical city, but it's crowded and full of all kinds of people. Besides," she added, "I had another motive; I wanted to see if anyone recognised you from your previous time here, when you first left Kanarzand."

Aidan raised an eyebrow. "A price on my head?"

Ahlissa nodded. "There was. But there isn't any more. Still, you never know who might be interested in you, even now. That's why I wanted to bring you back here, to see if any threats still linger."

Aidan, reflecting on her words, felt a twinge of doubt. Was I just being used? he wondered.

Ahlissa caught the look on his face and immediately responded. "Wait a moment. I know what you're thinking, and you're wrong. Don't for a second believe I want something to happen to you. I feel protective toward you. And as it turns out, nobody presented a threat. I doubt there's any danger toward you any more."

"Except maybe the woman who watched us leave last night," Aidan muttered. "And when I saw her on the dance floor, she turned away and didn't look at me again. So, she's no competition."

"Indeed," Ahlissa said, her tone lightening. "Was she attractive?"

Aidan hesitated before answering. "Yes. But that's all."

"Then why didn't you go to her?" Ahlissa teased, a playful glint in her eyes.

"Because I was in the company of you," Aidan said simply, his voice soft but sincere.

Ahlissa smiled warmly. "I see."

They finished their breakfast, the conversation shifting to lighter topics. As they prepared to leave the room, Aidan noticed something curious. The young woman from the previous night, the one who had been watching him so intently, was also leaving a room two doors down. She was in the company of a tall, blonde man dressed in fine clothes. They all arrived at the elevator together, sharing the ride down to the lobby.

The atmosphere in the elevator was awkward. Aidan could feel the woman's eyes on him again, and the sensation made the hair on the back of his neck rise. It was almost as if he could feel her breath on his skin, and it made him uneasy.

As they exited the elevator, the woman accidentally brushed past him, and Aidan felt a slight tug at his waistcoat. Glancing down, he realised she had slipped something into his pocket; a small, folded piece of paper. The woman glanced back at him, her expression apologetic.

"Forgive me," she said softly. "I'm sorry."

Aidan nodded, his heart pounding slightly. As he looked into her eyes, he noticed something unusual about them. They were lavender with gold flecks; an oddity that sparked a flicker of recognition in his mind.

As the couple walked away, Ahlissa, ever perceptive, turned to Aidan. "What was that about?" she asked, her voice cautious.

"Can we talk somewhere private?" Aidan replied, his voice low.

"Of course. Let's find a quiet booth in the dining area."

Once seated in a secluded corner of the lobby, Aidan explained his suspicions to Ahlissa. "The woman... there's something off about her. Her eyes were lavender with gold flecks. We both know Jillian is the only other person with eyes like that, so I think she might be another Khystar."

Ahlissa frowned, intrigued. "Khystar? Are you sure?"

Aidan nodded, pulling out the note from his pocket and unfolding it. The message was written in Khestar, the ancient tongue of the Aystaran people:

"We share something in common. I know of the mark you bear and may be able to help you uncover its power. When you are next in Gideon, you can locate me at the Broken Blade Inn. Ask the proprietor for me, and we can talk.

- Jillian"

Ahlissa's eyebrows shot up as she read the note over Aidan's shoulder. "Well, isn't that interesting? Could it really be Jillian? We believed her to be the last of her kind."

"How did she know about my mark?" Aidan mused. "If that's even what she's referring to."

"That's the real question," Ahlissa said. "We're new arrivals in Gideon. No one could have known to expect us. It seems unlikely that anyone here would already be aware of your mark."

Aidan leaned back, deep in thought. "Could it be possible that, as the guardian recognised me for being related to the ancient race at the ruins, this woman is somehow connected to that lineage too?"

Ahlissa studied him carefully. "Are you suggesting she thinks you're related to Khystar? As far as we know, your bloodline isn't connected to anything like that."

Aidan's mind drifted back to the history he had read about the Kale Ashtari in the ruins. Can Kale Ashtari change form? Yes, they could. They possessed the ability to appear as anything they chose, a skill they had perfected through magical means rather than it being an inherent racial trait. It was possible, then, that the Kale Ashtari might be considered shapeshifters, at least in a technical sense.

"Her race came from another world," Aidan began, speaking slowly as he worked through his thoughts. "I am of a lesser bloodline related to the Kale Ashtari, meaning my people also came from another world. I think we should meet her. She might have answers."

Ahlissa shook her head, her expression turning serious. "I advise against rushing into this. Think about the world we're in. This woman - potentially another shapeshifter - could be working for someone else, perhaps someone with more sinister motives. It could be a trap."

Aidan considered her words. "She did say 'when I next return.' Maybe I could leave a note, saying I'll meet her in six days or something."

"That could work," Ahlissa agreed. "But before we do anything, I suggest we investigate. I'll have some... associates look into the inn and see if there's anything suspicious."

Aidan nodded. "Yes, I'd feel better if we checked things out first. I'd like to know if she's being watched too. We know the Seeker is searching for another marked individual."

"Exactly," Ahlissa said. "And if Jillian does have a mark, as her note implies, then this could be a ploy to capture both of you."

"Let's return to the Zephyr Breeze," Aidan said, standing from the booth. "We need to get moving if we're going to make that delivery on time."

Ahlissa nodded. "Let's go."

Back on the Zephyr Breeze, Aidan changed into a crew uniform and made his way to the bridge. The ship had already undocked from the airship station and was moving west of Gideon City at a leisurely pace. Despite the size of the ship, its movement was fluid and silent, a testament to the advanced propulsion systems that continued to impress Aidan.

When Aidan arrived on the bridge, Ahlissa greeted him with a smile. "I'm glad you're here. I want to show you something." She motioned to a blank screen on the wall and tapped a smooth control panel. The screen flickered to life, revealing a colourful map with glowing markers.

"This is our current position," she said, pointing to a green dot that represented the Zephyr Breeze. "And this," she continued, indicating a blue dot Northwest of Gideon, "is our first waypoint. We're headed to an archaeological site in the desert. We've been tasked by the Seeker and the Gatherer to retrieve a consignment of artifacts they're interested in."

Aidan studied the map. "I don't recognise the location."

Ahlissa nodded. "It's a remote site. According to what we know, there are some artifacts there related to the Khestar civilization. Additionally, there are remains of an Argar-like creature the Seeker wants us to bring back. Our instructions are simple; retrieve the packaged consignment and return it to Gideon. I've asked no questions beyond that."

Aidan frowned. "This desert seems endless."

Ahlissa laughed. "It feels that way, doesn't it? But don't worry, one day we'll venture beyond it."

She pressed another button on the control panel, and a second blue dot appeared on the map. "This is our second waypoint. It's near Sindarr, and we're to deliver a special consignment to a man named Mhorvaeus. The boxes are marked 'fragile' and 'ornaments,' but I'm certain they contain Dark Aethyr shards."

Aidan raised an eyebrow. "Dark Aethyr shards?"

"Yes," Ahlissa replied. "I'm not asking too many questions about what they're for. My concern is ensuring Mhorvaeus pays us. I may need your help during negotiations, just in case things get complicated."

"Of course," Aidan said. "How can I assist?"

"You can listen for any languages they speak among themselves. If they're planning anything underhanded, you'll know."

Aidan nodded. "I look forward to helping you and the crew."

As the sun rose higher in the sky, the Zephyr Breeze picked up speed, gliding effortlessly over the sand dunes. After about an hour, they descended toward a cluster of large dunes and arrived at the first waypoint.

The sight that greeted them was remarkable; a large section of a metal object, possibly a ship, protruded from an embankment. The Zephyr Breeze hovered just above the ground, and a team of archaeologists and labourers stood waiting with several crates ready to be loaded.

"Welcome to Site 41," an archaeologist greeted them as they prepared to land.

13

Site 41

The Zephyr Breeze's aft hold began to fill with the large crates as the labourers' swiftly moved the precious cargo aboard. Each box was handled with care, their importance evident by the thoroughness with which they were secured in place by the crew. Aidan, dressed as a crew member, worked alongside them, ensuring the boxes were stabilized and locked down properly to prevent any damage during the airship's high-speed journey. The hold now carried more than just artifacts; it was heavy with the mysteries that lay within each crate; secrets unearthed from beneath the sands.

When the final box was safely stored, the Chief Archaeologist, Kalnar Cordovar, invited everyone to the campsite for light refreshments. Aidan, seeing the rest of the crew remove their desert masks, followed suit. The air was still dry and warm as he disembarked with Ahlissa and the others, following them toward a cluster of mauve-coloured tents nestled in a wide ravine. The tents stood like small fortresses against the harsh desert winds, sheltering the artifacts, researchers, and knowledge the expedition had unearthed over many months.

Ahlissa walked close to Aidan as they moved. "We are known here," she whispered. "You don't need to hide your identity. Our presence is no secret, and I think you'll find what these people discuss quite interesting."

"How long have they been here?" Aidan asked, taking in the scope of the operation.

"About twenty months," Ahlissa replied, glancing around as if mentally calculating how much had changed since her last visit.

Aidan nodded thoughtfully, his curiosity piqued. This wasn't just an ordinary dig site. The sheer number of artifacts being transported and the hushed secrecy surrounding the location spoke of something much more significant. He followed Ahlissa toward the centre of the camp, where the archaeologists were already gathering.

Kalnar Cordovar, a distinguished and accomplished Adeni man, stood at the head of the group, his weathered face lit by the glow of a nearby lantern. His eyes, though tired from months of intense work, sparkled with excitement as he greeted them. "Friends, you are most welcome! Lady Ahlissa, I must thank you again for helping us transport our discoveries back to Gideon City. It's always a pleasure to have the Zephyr Breeze assist us."

"The pleasure is mine," Ahlissa replied with a nod. "Your research is highly regarded by the Seeker and the Gatherer. We're honoured to be part of such important work."

Kalnar raised a glass filled with a light yellow, fruit-flavoured drink and smiled. "Here's to our continued success and discovery! To good health and knowledge!"

The assembled group raised their glasses in unison. Aidan took a sip and felt the refreshing sweetness tingle on his tongue, a pleasant contrast to the dry desert air. The archaeologists mingled with the crew, discussing their findings and speculating on what the buried ship might reveal next.

As the conversations flowed around him, Aidan felt a little out of place, unsure of how to contribute. Though he had learned much from his studies, the lively discussion between the archaeologists about ancient civilizations and mysterious artifacts was beyond his usual depth. He stood quietly, observing, trying to piece together the importance of what was unfolding here.

Tanith, a half-Aystar crew member who had been friendly with Aidan since his arrival on the Zephyr Breeze, noticed his isolation and wandered over to his side. "Hey," she greeted warmly. "You look a little lost. This must all feel new to you, right?"

Aidan smiled sheepishly. "Yeah, I've been out of touch with the world for a long time. It's all a bit overwhelming."

"Don't worry," Tanith reassured him. "This place is safe for us. We've been here since the first expedition arrived from Cordovar College to investigate an anomaly detected in the sands. We were the ones who evacuated them when the darkness fell over Kanarzand. It's only recently that they've been able to return and resume their work."

Aidan's curiosity deepened. "An anomaly?"

Tanith nodded, her eyes bright with enthusiasm. "Yes. Buried beneath this ravine is a massive metal vessel. Much larger and more advanced than the Zephyr Breeze. Only part of it has been uncovered so far, but from what we've seen, it's an ancient structure; possibly Khestar in origin."

Aidan's brow furrowed. "Khestar? I have been learning about them in my studies, but my understanding of them is incomplete."

"They were very real," Tanith said. "The Khestar were believed to be like the Aystar; but they were beings from another world. They came to this planet long ago. There's another site, Deck Nine, that was thought to be connected to them, but it was destroyed when Izen'draazt arrived. We believe there are other sites scattered across the world, each holding secrets of their technology and influence."

Aidan listened carefully, his mind racing with the possibilities. "I've visited a site where I think the Khestar once lived," he said, his voice quiet as he remembered the ruins he had explored. "The name they went by there was Kale Ashtari."

Tanith's eyes widened. "Kale Ashtari? I'll have to investigate that. It could be a term we haven't yet uncovered in the historical records. Maybe we'll find more clues in the libraries of Kharadia."

"I did see some references to the Khestar in my time there," Aidan agreed. "But my time was split between learning more about my people at the Temple of Ages and my martial lore training with the war clans of the Kale Khestari."

"Yes," Tanith explained. "Kharadia is where many of the oldest libraries are. Some are presided over by the Deathless Ones, the Kale Ereshkigal, our revered ancestors. If there are any answers to be found about the Kale Ashtari, that's where we'll likely find them."

Aidan nodded, feeling more connected to the mystery now. "This group existed during the Age of Darkness. They travelled to Scylla from the Eternal Void."

"That's fascinating!" Tanith exclaimed, genuinely intrigued. "I must confess, I'm a bit of a history buff, but I've never formally studied at the colleges in Kharadia. Sometimes I regret that."

She grabbed another drink from a nearby table and downed it quickly. "Well, enjoy yourself," she said with a smile. "I'm going to go mingle with the others. If you ever want to talk history, you know where to find me."

Aidan smiled as she walked away, feeling more at ease now. The world felt both vast and intimate at that moment. He was beginning to understand that history wasn't something trapped in dusty books; it was alive and unfolding around him.

After about an hour of relaxing at the camp, Ahlissa thanked the Chief Archaeologist for his hospitality and gathered the crew back aboard the Zephyr Breeze. The airship was soon skimming across the sand dunes at a low altitude, moving with a speed and grace that never ceased to amaze Aidan. On the bridge, Ahlissa was at ease, monitoring their course as the airship flew north.

After some time, she turned to Aidan, who had been standing quietly by the window, watching the desert pass beneath them. "Did you find

Site 41 intriguing?" she asked with a knowing smile.

"Yes, very much so," Aidan replied, still processing everything he had learned.

Ahlissa leaned back in her chair, her expression softening. "It's a special place. I've been involved with it since the beginning, partly because I was the one entrusted to take the original expedition there. The leader of that expedition... he was a good man. I keep coming back to honour him."

Aidan looked at her, sensing a deeper story. "What happened to him?"

"He died inside the artefact," Ahlissa said quietly. "Against the advice of his team, he entered it, believing he could unlock its secrets. But it was a trap. He was disintegrated instantly. The Seeker and the Gatherer believe Site 41 holds secrets that could offer Gideon protection, like how they defended the city against Izen'draazt's advance. The Thirteen are skilled in magic, but they believe the Progenitors used something different; something even more powerful. They want to harness that power to augment their magic."

Aidan nodded, understanding the stakes. "The defence of Gideon City was remarkable. But I remember the Wasteland Druid and his Sentinels played a major part as well."

"Yes," Ahlissa agreed. "It was a joint effort. We're all trying to figure out how to prevent another catastrophe like that. Site 41 might be the key."

As the conversation lulled, Aidan helped the crew where he could, assisting with minor tasks as the Zephyr Breeze soared north across the vast desert. As dusk began to fall, the landscape below changed. The barren dunes gave way to arid grasslands and low hills. The airship's speed slowed as they approached the edge of the desert.

One of the crew members approached Ahlissa with a report. "We've reached the border where the Tahnaar Desert ends, and the Kalos Plains begin. Lake Glassmere is directly ahead."

Ahlissa nodded and adjusted their course. "We'll skirt around the eastern side of the lake," she told Aidan. As they passed over a sprawling settlement built into rocky outcroppings, she gestured toward it. "That's Everhold. It's the largest settlement of the Adeni tribes that roam the Kalos Plains. They're fierce, proud, and independent people. They have a strong bond with the terror lizards that roam these lands. They believe those creatures give them strength in combat."

Aidan looked down at the settlement, curious. "What would they think of us flying over them?"

"They know who we are," Ahlissa replied. "The Adeni tribes recognise the Zephyr Breeze, and while we don't trade with them often, they know we carry supplies. Still, they're distrustful of strangers. Everhold is more a gathering of tribes than a permanent settlement. Its population constantly changes."

She pointed west, where a swirling gray mist loomed ominously. "We're also avoiding the Scornland. It's a dangerous place; destroyed by horrific magic during the Age of Calamity. The land itself is cursed. Any survivors of that cataclysm have been twisted into monsters. Healing magic doesn't work there, and the entire area is prone to violent magical storms. It's not a place anyone with sense would venture into."

Aidan studied the mist in the distance, feeling a chill run down his spine. "What caused it to become like that?"

"Powerful, unchecked magic," Ahlissa said grimly. "The Scornland was once a jewel, a thriving region. But when the cataclysm struck, it became an open grave. Nothing there is as it should be."

Ahlissa ordered the crew to descend and bring the Zephyr Breeze to rest among the hills, a few miles east of Everhold. "We'll rest here for the night," she announced. "All hands will remain on board, and I want a constant watch. It's possible one of the Adeni tribes has spotted us and might want to investigate. If they approach without hostility, we'll avoid contact. However, be on alert for any large predators; particularly large reptiles. If we must, we'll defend ourselves, but we cannot harm one of their sacred beasts. If we do, the Adeni will never forgive us."

Aidan volunteered for the night watch and was assigned a shift from midnight to four in the morning. The ship settled in behind the hills, and the crew rotated shifts to keep an eye on the perimeter.

The night passed without incident. Aidan, standing on the deck during his watch, gazed out over the moonlit plains, his mind wandering back to the events of the past few days. There were so many mysteries - both personal and historical - that he had yet to unravel. But one thing was certain: whatever lay ahead, he would face it with the same determination that had brought him this far.

The first light of dawn began to break over the horizon as Ahlissa appeared on deck, her sharp eyes scanning the landscape. "A quiet night?" she asked.

"Yes," Aidan replied. "No sign of any tribes or predators."

"Good," Ahlissa said, her voice calm but commanding. "We'll be moving out soon. The next leg of our journey awaits."

As the crew began preparing the airship for departure, Aidan felt a growing sense of anticipation. Whatever secrets lay hidden in the next waypoint, he was ready to uncover them.

14

Mhorvaeus

In the early morning light, Aidan found Ahlissa already awake and preparing for the next leg of their journey. She stood on the bridge of the Zephyr Breeze, her expression focused as she reviewed the navigation charts and adjusted their course.

"This day's travel will take us into Sindarr," she informed Aidan as he joined her. "We're ahead of schedule, which will certainly please Mhorvaeus."

Aidan noted the hint of caution in her voice. "You've mentioned him before. Do you trust him?"

Ahlissa shook her head slightly. "I've never met him before, so I'm cautious. Normally, I have a good sense of my clients before doing business, but this time is different. I need you to be on guard. I've already instructed the crew to ensure they're armed, and I advise you to do the same. And when we arrive, stay dressed like one of us... and wear the mask."

"Of course," Aidan replied without hesitation. He knew the drill by now. It was vital to maintain anonymity and blend in with the crew, especially in unknown territory. He returned to his quarters and made sure his gear was ready, fastening his magical longsword securely to his side. His mask, designed to obscure his features, was already waiting in his pack.

The day proceeded uneventfully, with the Zephyr Breeze gliding through the sky at high speed, flying parallel to the path of the spark rail guide stones below. The sight of the guide stones, stark and ancient, gave Aidan a strange sense of connection to the world beneath him - a world he was now seeing from above for the first time. It was exhilarating, this swift and silent travel, as the desert plains and towns passed beneath them like a shifting tapestry of life and history.

They passed over Ostarr, a large town, and soon, their destination came into view; a low stone tower and a walled compound nestled among hills about two miles from the town. The citadel of Mhorvaeus was secluded, fortified, and foreboding. Aidan couldn't shake the sense of unease that settled over him as the Zephyr Breeze descended.

As they landed, a dozen soldiers and an equal number of servants greeted them. The soldiers stood rigid, their expressions blank, while the servants quickly moved to assist with unloading the cargo.

A tall, imposing figure stepped forward, dressed in armour that gleamed in the midday sun. "Welcome to Mhorvaeus' citadel, Lady Ahlissa," the commander said with a formal bow. "I am Althas, Captain of the Guard. Lord Mhorvaeus is inside and awaits your arrival. Please, follow me."

Ahlissa motioned for Aidan and a dozen crew members to accompany her as they followed Althas. "Our servants will assist with the cargo delivery," Althas added as they passed through the raised portcullis and into the compound.

"Thank you," Ahlissa replied, her tone polite but guarded. "And how is your lord today?"

"Very well, my lady," Althas said as they crossed the courtyard, which was surrounded by outbuildings such as stables and storage areas. Everything seemed orderly, but Aidan felt a prickling sensation along the back of his neck. They were being watched; closely.

Once inside the tower, they were led through a set of double doors into a grand chamber. It was a magnificent room, with rich tapestries adorning the walls and soft, plush seating arranged around long tables laden with food and drink. At the far end, a man sat on a throne, dressed in fine purple robes. His appearance was striking; middle-aged, with chiselled features and a calm, almost regal demeanour.

Mhorvaeus rose as they entered, his arms open wide in a gesture of welcome. "Friends, you have arrived. I trust your journey was pleasant. I am Mhorvaeus. It is a privilege to meet you."

Ahlissa stepped forward, her movements smooth and composed. "I am Ahlissa," she introduced herself. "We have brought the consignment of boxes from Gideon, as requested. The journey was without incident."

"Excellent!" Mhorvaeus exclaimed, his voice warm. "Please, enjoy the food and drink. You've travelled far. Will you be staying the night?"

Aidan observed Mhorvaeus carefully, something about the man unsettling him. His manner was almost too polished, too welcoming. And there was something beneath that warm exterior; something much older than the face that smiled at them.

"Your offer is generous," Ahlissa replied, "but I regret we won't be staying. Once delivery is confirmed and payment received, we must depart immediately. There is additional business that requires my attention."

Mhorvaeus nodded, not missing a beat. "I understand completely," he said, his eyes gleaming. "My servants will bring payment shortly. But first, tell me, how is Gideon these days? Has it recovered from the terror Izen'draazt brought upon the region?"

Ahlissa's expression darkened slightly. "Slowly. The city was fortunate to have remained unscathed. The High Magocracy and the Wasteland Druid shielded it from the advancing evil."

Aidan's instincts were on high alert. There was something wrong here. The air in the room felt heavy, charged with an unnatural energy. He quietly called upon the Aethyr to inform him of the motives around him and immediately felt the overwhelming presence of malevolence. Mhorvaeus was indeed evil.

"Fortunate, indeed," Mhorvaeus mused. "Ornaments such as those you have procured on my behalf are becoming harder to obtain. But Gideon is an ancient place, with many secrets beneath its streets. Secrets I find... fascinating."

As they sat, Mhorvaeus gestured toward the lavish spread before them, and the conversation shifted to lighter topics; Gideon's architecture, the region's history, and the recent developments in trade. A string quartet played in the background, their delicate melodies filling the room.

Aidan remained silent for much of the conversation, his mind focused on Mhorvaeus's every move. When Mhorvaeus turned to speak quietly with one of his servants, Aidan strained to listen. The words were not in the common tongue but in a corrupted, forbidden language; the language of the dead.

He knows I'm listening, Aidan realised, as Mhorvaeus briefly glanced in his direction, his eyes narrowing slightly before continuing his conversation. The accent was thick, the dialect obscure; one Aidan had only seen referenced in a handful of ancient texts from the library at Kanarzand.

The conversation was brief, but Aidan caught enough. Mhorvaeus instructed his servants to ensure the payment was in order and to document everything they could about the Zephyr Breeze; its capabilities, its defences, anything that couldn't easily be explained as magical or natural. Mhorvaeus's interest in the airship was far more than casual. He was gathering information, perhaps for himself, perhaps for someone else.

Ahlissa noticed Aidan's distraction and, after a few more minutes of polite conversation, she excused herself. "Forgive me," she said with a graceful smile. "I need a moment outside."

"Of course," Mhorvaeus said, his voice smooth. He gestured toward the door. "Take as much time as you need."

Ahlissa motioned for Aidan to follow her, and they stepped out into the courtyard, the crisp air a welcome contrast to the stifling atmosphere inside the citadel. The guards watched them from a respectful distance, but Aidan knew they were listening closely.

"So?" Ahlissa asked softly. "Has he kept to our deal?"

Aidan nodded but spoke cautiously. "He will keep to the agreement. But he isn't Adeni. He's evil, and he speaks the language of the dead. He also had his people look over your ship; an opportunistic move, probably for himself or whoever he's working with. And he knows I understand the language he's speaking."

Ahlissa's expression tightened. "The language of the dead? That's... troubling. It's outlawed across most of Scylla. If Mhorvaeus is dabbling in that, we need to tread carefully. He may have ties to the Servants of Aroth."

Aidan's eyes narrowed. "Servants of Aroth? The vampire cult?"

"Yes," Ahlissa confirmed. "Aroth was the First Vampire. Her followers believe she will rise again and reclaim her throne. Lord Khannay, the benefactor of the library in Kanarzand, was one of her Servants. Mhorvaeus could be connected to that."

Aidan thought for a moment. "Mhorvaeus mentioned being interested in the underground of Gideon. If Khannay was involved, it would make sense for Mhorvaeus to have used him."

Ahlissa sighed, glancing at the guards. "We should assume this conversation is being monitored. We'll need to search the ship for anything out of place when we leave. If Mhorvaeus is working with the Servants of Aroth, we may be dealing with something far more dangerous than we thought."

Aidan nodded. "Agreed. Let's head back inside before he grows suspicious."

When they re-entered the chamber, Mhorvaeus greeted them with a smile, gesturing to three medium-sized wooden chests. "Your payment, as agreed; thirty thousand gold sovereigns."

Ahlissa nodded and motioned for her crew to collect the chests. "It was a pleasure doing business with you."

Mhorvaeus smiled, his eyes gleaming. "The pleasure was mine. Your airship is an impressive vessel. It serves you well."

"Yes," Ahlissa said with a small smile. "The Zephyr Breeze is freedom."

Mhorvaeus laughed, a low, throaty sound. "It's also known for bringing swift death to your enemies. Its reputation is legendary, especially your treatment of Kanarzand's Arcane Council."

Aidan stiffened at the mention of Kanarzand, but Ahlissa remained composed. "Reputations are hard to maintain these days."

"Indeed," Mhorvaeus said with a nod. "Perhaps we will do business again. I will recommend your services to my associates."

Ahlissa smiled politely, but Aidan could sense her discomfort. "Until we meet again."

As they departed, Aidan couldn't shake the feeling that Mhorvaeus had revealed more than he intended. Back on board the Zephyr Breeze, Ahlissa gave the order to lift off immediately. As the airship rose into the sky, she commanded the crew to inspect everything thoroughly for any signs of tampering or tracking.

Aidan returned to his quarters and searched through his belongings. Nothing seemed out of place. Still, the sense of unease from their encounter lingered, especially as the memory of Mhorvaeus's corrupted speech replayed in his mind. He lay down to rest but was haunted by nightmares, his chest burning with the familiar pain that accompanied his dreams. When he woke, the pain subsided, but the feeling of dread remained.

The next morning, Ahlissa found Aidan on the bridge, looking out over the horizon. "Did you sleep well?" she asked, though her tone suggested she already knew the answer.

"Restless," Aidan admitted.

"Was it the dream again?"

Aidan nodded. "It was the same as usual. But this time, it felt... different. I think hearing Mhorvaeus speak in that language triggered something."

Ahlissa's face tightened in concern. "You've been through a lot, Aidan. Maybe this encounter stirred up more than just memories."

"Maybe," Aidan said quietly. "But whatever Mhorvaeus is, he's dangerous. He knew I could understand him, and he let me hear him.

That was no accident."

Ahlissa agreed. "We'll have to be careful going forward. He expressed interest in doing more business, but something tells me that could be a double-edged sword."

Aidan nodded, his mind still racing with the implications of what had transpired. Mhorvaeus was playing a game - a dangerous one - and Aidan knew that their paths would cross again. He could only hope they would be ready when it happened.

As the Zephyr Breeze flew on towards Gideon City, Aidan resolved to learn more about Mhorvaeus, the Servants of Aroth, and the mysterious Undercity of Gideon.

15

The Broken Blade Inn

The Zephyr Breeze arrived over Gideon City with all precautions in place, its sleek form descending cautiously into the airship docks. As soon as the craft was moored, Aidan prepared to depart, carefully dressing in unremarkable clothing and securing his longsword in its scabbard with the customary peace tie. His destination, the Broken Blade inn, was known for attracting a rowdy crowd, and Aidan knew well that discretion would be paramount. Yet, for all his readiness, he sensed an extra weight in his steps as he prepared to leave.

Just as he reached the gangplank, Ahlissa approached him, her face marked with concern.

"Aidan," she called, catching his arm lightly. "Are you sure you're ready for this? The Broken Blade isn't known for its subtlety, and the crowd there is often... less than welcoming."

Aidan met her gaze, her worry softening his own expression. "I'll be fine. I know it's not the safest place, but I need to see what's happening there first hand."

"I know," she replied, exhaling. "But you must understand; there's a reason I assigned my agents to that inn. It's a hunting ground for those with scores to settle. There's risk, even for someone prepared." She paused, her grip tightening. "Don't think your presence there has gone unnoticed."

Aidan gave a slight nod, grateful for her caution but determined. "That's why I'm dressed as plainly as possible. And you already have agents stationed nearby, so I won't be alone, even if it looks that way."

Ahlissa's lips pressed into a thin line. "True. I have two operatives already embedded, and they'll be watching for any trouble. But I don't want to have to step in because something goes wrong." She looked away briefly, then back, her eyes fierce. "There's someone else at that inn who might recognise you, someone with a grudge."

Aidan met her gaze, sensing her unease. "Thaxos."

"Yes," Ahlissa confirmed, her tone dark. "That Argar brute and his band of mercenaries are notorious even here. The last thing you need is Thaxos recognising you in that den."

Aidan took a steadying breath. "I'll keep my head down. This isn't the first time I've faced Thaxos, and it probably won't be the last."

She seemed to consider his resolve before responding. "Remember, if you feel even the slightest hint of things getting out of control, leave. My agents will signal if it's too dangerous to continue. I won't risk you getting tangled up with his kind again."

Aidan offered her a reassuring smile, though he understood her worry.

"I know. And I appreciate your concern, Ahlissa. I won't take unnecessary risks."

With a final look, Ahlissa released his arm, nodding. "Go then. But be careful, Aidan. Thaxos may not be the only danger lurking there."

With a final nod, Aidan turned and made his way through the bustling streets of Gideon City toward the Pleasure Quarter. He wound his way past vendors, performers, and townsfolk, each adding their own lively, if somewhat chaotic, energy to the cityscape. Eventually, he reached the northern end of the city, where the Broken Blade inn stood opposite the main gate, its decrepit appearance and raucous sounds making it hard to miss.

The inn's name was reflected in the massive, shattered sword blade that hung above the entrance. The weapon, ancient and imposing, had likely belonged to a giant or some other powerful creature, now mounted like a grim trophy for all who dared enter. Aidan studied the sign for a moment, steeling himself. The sight of the inn's worn façade and the noise spilling out into the street did little to calm his nerves. This was a place where the rougher, often lawless types gathered, a place where tempers flared as quickly as they cooled, if they cooled at all.

Pushing the door open, Aidan stepped inside and was immediately hit by the stale air tinged with ale, smoke, and the faint but unmistakable scent of blood. The inn was packed, full of loud voices and boisterous laughter, the kind of crowd that would just as quickly cheer for a brawl as they would a good drink. His eyes roamed the room, noting the ruffians, mercenaries, and others who likely worked in various shades of legality.

In the dim light, his attention was drawn to a painting mounted on the far wall. There, the likeness of an Argar warrior stood out, one-eyed and ugly, dressed in fine mithril armour. Beneath the image, in dried, cracked blood, was scrawled, *"Thaxos, mighty warrior and mercenary. Not Farm Boy."* Aidan felt a chill run down his spine as he recognised the ugly wonky-eyed face; the same Thaxos who had sworn to hunt him down for disturbing their activities at the Mhargrave dig site, prior to the fall of Kanarzand.

Aidan's hand brushed instinctively against his longsword, but he quickly steadied himself, reminding himself that the peace tie was there for a reason. He moved carefully, finding an empty spot at a table near the edge of the room. Sitting with his back to the wall, he made sure to keep a clear view of the entrance and the painting of Thaxos, his mind racing with the implications of his presence.

He hadn't been there long before one of Ahlissa's undercover agents approached, slipping into the seat across from him under the pretence of being an old friend. The agent, a lean, wiry man with sharp eyes, nodded subtly in acknowledgment.

"Aidan," he muttered in a low voice, glancing around casually, "you're definitely not blending in here. Eyes are already on you, but we've got your back if things go south."

Aidan inclined his head slightly. "I noticed. Anything I should know?"

The agent hesitated briefly, then leaned in. "Word around here is that Thaxos and his crew are currently occupied outside the city limits. But his supporters? They're here. Most of the patrons here tonight would be more than happy to cause trouble if given the excuse. Watch yourself."

Aidan acknowledged the warning. "Understood. I'll make my inquiry and leave. This isn't the place to linger."

Just then, a pair of rugged men glanced his way, muttering to each other as they sized him up. Aidan kept his expression neutral, offering no reaction. The Broken Blade wasn't a place to show weakness, but it wasn't a place to flaunt strength either.

The agent nodded once more. "Good call. I'll be nearby, keeping an eye out. If you need an exit, follow my lead." With that, he gave Aidan a small, reassuring smile, rising as nonchalantly as he'd arrived.

Aidan took a deep breath, his gaze shifting back to the ominous painting of Thaxos. The Argar leader's painted face seemed to stare back, almost as though mocking his presence. Every sound in the rowdy inn was now amplified, every glance suspicious. He knew that his presence here was precarious, and any wrong move could draw attention he didn't want.

Still, with Ahlissa's agents nearby and his own resolve steeled, he focused on his purpose. He would gather what he came for quickly, and then he would leave, all the while mindful of the shadows shifting in the Broken Blade's dimly lit corners.

As Aidan considered his next move, he was immediately met by an unexpected jab to his left shoulder. The hand lingered there for a moment, heavy and deliberate, and Aidan could sense the tension in the air. A rough voice followed the jab, tinged with both mockery and intimidation.

"Who said your kind could come in here? We've got rules about pointy ears," the man sneered. "And by the look of 'em, yours are plenty pointy."

Aidan resisted the urge to roll his eyes as he turned, meeting the gaze of the towering figure. "Don't let that bother you," he replied smoothly. "These pointy ears grew up on the same streets of Gideon as you did." Without further comment, he continued to the bar, dismissing the confrontation as just another provocation.

The inn's patrons, who had been watching closely, fell into murmurs of amusement and approval. But the man wasn't satisfied.

"Oi! How dare you disrespect Odorous the Magnificent!" the hulking Argar bellowed, his fists clenched. "Turn and face me properly, half-breed!"

Reluctantly, Aidan turned and found himself staring up at a large, bare-chested Argar. The man loomed over him, his scowl deepening as he took in Aidan's casual stance. Just as Aidan tensed, preparing himself for what could become an ugly fight, another voice cut through the noise, strong and laced with authority.

"Stand down, Odorous. Let the half-breed Aystar enjoy his ale," called the voice from a side table.

Odorous snarled but obeyed, stepping back reluctantly. He cast Aidan one last dark look before retreating to a table where a group of rough-looking Adeni men sat, their faces unreadable but clearly taking note of the exchange. The man who had intervened gave Aidan a casual salute, grinning, before he resumed his conversation with his companions.

Aidan took his opportunity and approached the bar. He ordered an ale for himself and another for the man who had spoken up on his behalf, instructing the barkeep to deliver it. A young woman behind the bar, with a friendly if cautious smile, handed Aidan a tall tankard.

"This one's on the house," she said with a slight grin. "Name's Jenna. You're lucky. Odorous has crushed skulls for less. Just stay out of his way, and you'll be fine. I'll get that drink over to your friend."

Aidan raised his tankard in thanks. "Much appreciated, Jenna."

She gestured toward a side booth. "Why don't you take that spot? A little more privacy. And I'll bring you something to eat on the house; a spiced potato mash with meat and gravy. Our speciality."

Aidan hesitated. "I'd like to pay for it, actually."

She raised an eyebrow and shrugged. "Suit yourself."

Settling into the booth, Aidan took in his surroundings. The inn was as loud as it was dim, the kind of place that carried stories of all kinds in the shadows and whispers. Shortly, Remus, a lanky server with an easy gait, approached with a steaming plate of food. "Here you are, sir," he said, setting down the meal.

Aidan nodded his thanks, the aroma of spices and gravy reminding him of how hungry he was. He dug in, appreciating the hearty meal, and had almost finished when the door creaked open. A trio of men entered the inn, dressed in identical black shirts and wide-brimmed hats. A ripple of unease swept through the room. Patrons began to leave with murmurs of unease, draining the lively energy from the room.

Jenna, noticing the shift in atmosphere, signalled Remus. He hurriedly prepared drinks and food for the newcomers, who took a seat near the centre of the inn. Aidan observed them, noting how patrons averted their eyes, keeping their distance. These men needed no weapons to project authority; fear alone seemed their chosen weapon.

Finishing his meal, Aidan flagged Remus to clear the table. "Everything alright, sir?" Remus asked, his tone respectful. "Would you be needing a room?"

Aidan shook his head. "No, thanks. But give my compliments to the cook. The food was excellent."

Remus dipped his head in acknowledgment. "Thank you, Master Aidan. I'll pass it along."

He lingered for a moment before leaning in. "We were holding a message from Jillian, or rather, a note for someone named Aidan, but it's been misplaced. However, a young woman, fitting the description, has been staying here. Room 23 upstairs. She hasn't been seen for a few days; not since those men arrived."

Aidan's eyes narrowed as he glanced over at the three men. "And these men? Who are they?"

Remus shifted uncomfortably. "They're called the Observers. They've been moving from inn to inn across Gideon. No one dares challenge them. Last time someone did - a rough sort named Mangle - they immobilized him with just a word. The Sentinel Guards came for him, and no one's seen him since."

Aidan digested the information carefully, glancing once more at the Observers. Their presence was as unsettling as the silence they seemed to draw around them. "I was supposed to meet her tonight," he said quietly, "but with them here, I'll need to be cautious."

Remus nodded, producing a small brass key. "Room 23. Take a look for yourself if you need to. Just be careful. I can arrange for you to stay here as well if that would make it easier."

Considering his options, Aidan decided it was best to have a room in case he needed to blend in or lie low for a while. "Thank you, Remus. I'll take it. Could I have one on the second floor?"

Jenna promptly handed him the key to Room 13, her face shadowed with concern. The Observers didn't seem to be interested in him, but they were watching, and the tension they exuded hung in the room like a fog. Aidan kept his movements casual, slipping away from the bar and making his way upstairs without a backward glance, his mind already racing with what he might find in Room 23.

At the top of the stairs, he stopped outside the room, turning the key slowly in the lock, hoping to find some trace of the woman he'd been meant to meet. The quiet hallway seemed to echo with every sound, heightening his anticipation.

The small room was simply furnished, with only a modest bed, a small writing desk, and an adjoining wash room. After confirming that everything was secure, Aidan turned his thoughts back to his mission and climbed the stairs to the third floor, unlocking Room 23 with deliberate caution.

The room was sparsely decorated, yet carefully maintained. Only a few personal effects were scattered about, suggesting that Jillian - or Jilathraen, as he now knew her - had left in haste or perhaps had never intended to stay long. The wardrobe held an assortment of clothing: fine leather boots, a few dark dresses, and men's shirts that seemed deliberately inconspicuous, designed for blending into crowds. On the dresser, he spotted two scroll cases, one of which contained the letter he had written to her. The other, however, bore strange markings and symbols.

Aidan gently removed the scroll from its case, holding it carefully as he unfurled it. The symbols were intricate, an elaborate script that felt almost musical in its rhythm, yet he struggled to make sense of them. Summoning his magical abilities, he cast a spell of comprehension. The symbols shifted into legible text, revealing a letter written in ancient Khystar. The letter addressed Jillian by her true name, "Jilathraen," and spoke of the mountain sanctuaries of Aldrosia, a refuge for the Khystar people against the "Zealots of the Dreamlands." It also warned of a dark force known as the Aspiring Dream and urged her people to conceal themselves in Scylla to avoid its influence.

Aidan felt a strange unease settle over him as he absorbed the letter's contents. Until now, he had assumed that Jillian was simply a skilled shapeshifter, someone on the run and hiding from the prejudice and bigotry of the High Magocracy. But this letter hinted at something far deeper; something ancient and rooted in another world. Jillian wasn't a mere fugitive; she was a Khystar, a member of an enigmatic race believed to have originated from Kharadia and the Eternal Void. Aidan realised that this explained her knowledge of the Aethyr Marks, despite the fact that the Khystar were not known to bear them. The revelation left him with more questions than answers.

135

Setting the scroll aside, Aidan penned a quick note in Khystar, address-ing her by her true name. "*Read the message. I'll wait in Room 13 until tomorrow.*" As he placed the note on the dresser, a chill ran down his spine; a visceral sensation of being watched.

He spun around, and there, materializing from the shadows, was Jillian. Her lavender eyes caught the low light of the room, flecked with gold, and her gaze was steady, almost amused.

"Hello, Aidan," she said softly, her voice a melodic whisper. "I see you've learned some of my people's language. Impressive. You've made quite the effort to find me."

Aidan met her gaze, surprised yet not entirely unnerved by her sudden appearance.

"Remus gave me your key," he replied, lifting his letter to her in his hand. "I found this - and your letter."

Jillian nodded. "Remus is loyal and trustworthy," she said, her tone laced with approval.

"I imagine you're curious as to why I left you that cryptic note back at the Liberty Spire."

"I am," Aidan admitted. "Especially after reading what I just found."

Jillian's gaze softened, an expression of understanding and perhaps a hint of weariness.

"It's rare for a Khystar to reach out, let alone contact someone marked as you are. I sense the journey you've been on has not been an easy one. The taint you carry - your Aethyr Mark - has affected you deeply, hasn't it? I can offer you a way to diminish its discomfort, if that's something you desire."

Aidan hesitated, reflecting on the unsettling sensations that had been plaguing him; the pulsing discomfort, the vivid dreams. "The taint... it causes pain, yes, but it's also granted me knowledge I wouldn't have discovered otherwise. I sensed you might understand. You said we have something in common. What did you mean?"

Jillian's expression turned pensive. "We share an origin... in darkness," she said, her voice barely a whisper. "My people, the Khystar, were born after the Kale Ashtari were tainted by dark spirits. We've spent centuries moving toward the Strands of Light, but remnants of that darkness remain. In you, I sense a familiar trace, a shadow rooted in your lineage. The first of my people were not kind. In truth, they sought to enslave my ancestors. But you; you resist that darkness, even as it tries to consume you."

Her words echoed through him, stirring memories of his recent trials. "Yes, the Aethyr Mark brings pain, but it's a path I believe I'm meant to follow. It's as if this mark - this taint - binds me to a destiny."

Jillian nodded. "Then it's clear you feel the call just as I do. I carry a mark myself," she said, revealing a faint, serpentine symbol that curled along her wrist. She traced it in the air, the shape mirroring a pattern he had seen before.

"Interesting," Aidan murmured, his eyes tracing her mark. "I saw symbols like this during my time at the Kale Ashtari outpost. They seem connected, as if they've been guiding us, marking us."

Jillian sighed, her gaze drifting briefly toward the door. "Symbols of this kind are what draw the Observers to us, those men downstairs. They've been following me, hunting for any marked individuals."

Aidan's brow furrowed in concern. "They're scouring the city for anyone bearing Aethyr Marks. I think I can get you to safety. Ahlissa's airship, the Zephyr Breeze, is trustworthy. She's offered me refuge, and I believe she'd extend the same to you."

Jillian regarded him thoughtfully, her eyes studying his face. "Are you certain of this? You barely know me."

"Ahlissa knows about my Aethyr Mark," Aidan replied firmly. "She's helped protect me, even when she didn't fully understand it."

For a moment, Jillian's expression was unreadable. Then she nodded slowly, a hint of relief visible in her eyes. "Very well," she said. "I'll go with you. Meet me on the second-floor landing at dawn. Five a.m. sharp."

Aidan handed her the key to Room 13. "If anything happens before then, I'll be waiting here. Just be careful."

Jillian's smile was faint but sincere. "Thank you, Aidan. Rest well tonight and be on guard."

He watched her fade into the shadows of the room, her presence dissipating as quietly as she had arrived. With a sense of purpose mixed with apprehension, Aidan left her room and returned to his own, his steps cautious. He couldn't shake the feeling that the Observers' watchful eyes were on him as he moved.

16

The Observers

Aidan listened, footsteps echoing faintly from the dim corridor. The approaching steps were slow, almost methodical, each one heavy and deliberate. His body tensed as a figure emerged from the shadows. It was one of the three men who had been seated in the far corner of the bar earlier. This stranger's eyes were unlike any he'd seen before; cold, depthless black, like staring into an endless void. The inky darkness of his gaze sent an instinctive chill through Aidan.

"Nice evening for a walk, isn't it?" the stranger remarked, his voice a low, gravelly rumble that carried an edge of something sinister.

"It is indeed," Aidan replied smoothly, holding the man's gaze with deliberate calm, determined not to show his apprehension.

The stranger didn't respond immediately. He simply stared at Aidan, his black eyes unwavering, as if studying him for signs of fear or weakness. Without a word, he finally turned and continued down the hallway, heading toward the staircase. Aidan exhaled, the weight of the man's presence lingering in the air like a thick fog. Moving forward, Aidan heard the stranger's heavy, deliberate footsteps behind him, shadowing his every step as they descended together.

At the bar, Aidan ordered a drink; just a refreshing ale, hoping the familiar warmth of it might settle his nerves. His senses, however, stayed heightened. He could feel the three strangers' eyes fixed on him, even as they murmured amongst themselves at their table. Whatever their whispered conversation entailed, their gaze remained trained on him, each glance charged with tension.

Jenna, the bartender, leaned forward slightly, her brow creased in worry. "Looks like those guys don't like you," she murmured, her voice barely audible over the low hum of the inn.

Aidan gave a small shrug, his voice carrying enough to be heard by the strangers. "Too bad for them."

Jenna's eyes darted back to the trio, her concern evident. "Just...be careful," she said quietly. "They don't mess around. You don't want to be on their bad side, trust me."

Before Aidan could reply, one of the three men rose from the table, striding over to the bar with an air of purpose. He stopped next to Aidan, saying nothing for a moment as he stared intently at Jenna. His face was stony, unreadable, until he finally spoke.

"Another Dragonbolt," he ordered bluntly. "Two more for my friends, and one for this guy too." He jerked a thumb toward Aidan. "We'd like to see what he's made of."

Jenna gave a slight, resigned shrug and poured the drinks, sliding them across the counter. "Whatever you say, fella," she muttered.

The man grabbed three of the drinks, pushing the fourth toward Aidan with a challenging smile. "Drink up, boy. It's a gift," he said, his voice dripping with condescension as he watched Aidan expectantly.

Aidan glanced at the small, brimming glass in front of him, recognising it immediately. Dragonbolt was a potent distilled spirit, notorious for its fiery kick and infamous for flooring even the most seasoned drinkers. He hesitated, aware that this "gift" was less about hospitality and more about testing his limits. His instincts told him this wasn't just a casual invitation; it was a challenge, a power play.

The man's smug grin faded into a sneer. "What's wrong? Got a problem with that?"

Aidan met his gaze calmly. "Yes," he replied coolly, "you didn't ask."

The stranger's sneer deepened, his eyes narrowing. "Didn't ask what? Whether you've got the stomach for it, or if you're too weak to handle it? Like I said, it's a gift. Take it or leave it; doesn't matter to me. I just figured you ain't got what it takes."

Without waiting for Aidan's response, the man turned and walked back to his table, leaving the Dragonbolt untouched on the bar.

Jenna looked from the drink to Aidan, her worry plain. "You'd better watch yourself," she warned in a low tone, glancing nervously at the men. "They're marking you. I don't know what their interest is, but they don't go after just anyone."

Aidan leaned in, his voice barely a whisper. "Don't worry, they're being watched too. Thanks, Jenna. Good night."

With that, he left the Dragonbolt where it sat and headed for the door, fully aware of the three pairs of eyes burning into his back as he walked away. He didn't give them the satisfaction of looking back, maintaining a casual stride until he stepped outside and let the cool night air envelop him.

The dark streets were nearly empty, save for the muted bustle of a few scattered passer-by. He moved quickly, though not hurriedly, his senses sharp as he listened for any sign of pursuit. He knew enough about the type to recognise when he was being trailed, and the atmosphere in the inn had been thick with a latent hostility. It was only a matter of time before they'd try to confront him.

As he rounded a corner, Aidan's mind raced. Who were these men, and why were they so intent on sizing him up? If they were Observers, as he suspected, their interest could be tied to his Aethyr Mark. And if that were the case, his next move would have to be even more calculated.

He kept to the shadows, moving through the narrow alleys as he put distance between himself and the inn. Each footfall seemed amplified in the stillness, his heightened vigilance making even the smallest sounds feel ominous. But he pressed on, resolving to reach the Zephyr Breeze and seek Ahlissa's counsel. She needed to know about this new threat. She'd been an invaluable ally so far, and if anyone could help him navigate the dangers that seemed to be closing in, it was her.

The route took him through an old marketplace, its stalls and shops closed for the night. The shadows cast by the empty structures added an eerie quality to the scene, but he found reassurance in the familiar path. As he neared the edge of the square, he sensed a presence behind him, silent and watchful. His pace quickened, slipping into the alleyways leading to the docks.

After several minutes of careful navigation, he arrived at the Zephyr Breeze's berth. Ahlissa was waiting at the gangplank, her posture calm but her eyes scanning the area with the practiced sharpness of a seasoned operative.

"Aidan," she greeted, her voice low, laced with a hint of concern. "Everything alright?"

"Not exactly," he admitted, keeping his voice steady. "There were three men in the inn; Observers, I think. They've taken an unhealthy interest in me. We need to be careful."

Ahlissa nodded, her gaze hardening. "Observers don't pick targets lightly. If they're interested in you, it's only a matter of time before they escalate." She gave him a measured look. "I'll tighten security on board. They won't get close to you here. Get some rest, Aidan. We'll be ready if they come knocking."

With a quiet word of thanks, he boarded the Zephyr Breeze, the familiar embrace of the ship's hold offering a brief reprieve from the night's tension, for a few hours.

In the cool, pre-dawn stillness, Aidan returned and moved quietly through the inn's upper corridor, his eyes scanning every corner as he approached the landing. At precisely 5 a.m., he found Jillian waiting in the shadows, her form barely discernible in the dim light. She was dressed simply, her demeanour composed but with an unmistakable tension about her.

"Are you ready?" he asked in a low voice, glancing at her minimal belongings. "Did you get everything you need?"

Jillian nodded, her face calm but resolute. "I travel lightly," she replied softly, and there was a subtle strength in her voice. She carried little with her but wore a quiet determination as she prepared to leave behind the life she had led on the run.

Together, they descended the staircase, moving quickly but quietly through the inn's shadowed halls. At the bar, Jenna was wiping down tables, her tired eyes flickering with curiosity as she noticed the two approaching. Remus, who had been sweeping up near the door, paused to nod a farewell.

"Keep the room key," Jenna said to Jillian with a warm smile. "You've paid up for another fortnight if you need it."

Jillian returned the nod, murmuring her thanks before stepping out onto the quiet city street. The air was cool and fresh, a welcome contrast to the stifling tension they had felt inside the inn. With the city still under the early morning hush, they made their way through the cobbled streets. Public transport was sparse but reliable at that hour, and soon they boarded a sky carriage that would take them directly to the Skybridge, the main airship facility in Gideon City. The morning fog lingered around the rooftops as the city slowly came to life.

As they approached the gangway of the Zephyr Breeze, Aidan spotted Ahlissa overseeing the morning preparations, her form a steady presence among the bustling crew. She noticed him immediately and gave a wave, her smile widening when she saw Jillian at his side.

"Hey, Aidan!" she called out, making her way over with her usual ease. She looked Jillian over, her eyes sparkling with a hint of mischief. "And who's this fine young friend of yours?" she asked, nodding approvingly at Jillian. "She's pretty; much nicer than your usual catch!"

Aidan flushed, caught off guard. "What? I'm not - she's not -" he stammered, feeling his cheeks burn as Ahlissa's grin widened.

Jillian chuckled softly, giving him a sympathetic look. "I see you haven't changed, Aidan," she said, patting his arm.

Ahlissa laughed and offered Jillian her hand. "What's your name, then?"

With a quick nod, Jillian transformed into her previous appearance from her first journey aboard the Zephyr Breeze. "You already know me, Ahlissa. I'm Jilathraen," she said, her voice carrying a touch of formality. "But friends call me Jillian. I'm Aidan's contact from the Broken Blade. He sent me a letter, and I waited, as he requested."

Ahlissa raised an eyebrow, glancing between the two with newfound respect. "Well, I'm impressed. Aidan, handy with a quill and paper; it's nice to know he's good for more than reading dusty old books." She winked at him. "In fact, he's rather handy in general."

Jillian's expression softened as she added, "He's also very brave. I heard he stood up to several Observers at the inn last night. He didn't let them get the better of him."

"Really?" Ahlissa asked, her tone shifting from amusement to interest. "So, who were these Observers?"

Aidan shrugged. "Three men with an unsettling presence. They didn't exactly introduce themselves, but I got the sense they're keeping an eye on more than just the usual riff-raff around the city. They'd been watching Jillian and me for some time. I didn't let them provoke me, but it's clear they're more dangerous than the average troublemakers."

Ahlissa's smile faded, her gaze becoming focused. "The Observers are serious players, Aidan. If they're interested in you, we need to keep our guard up." She turned her attention back to Jillian, her eyes sharp yet kind. "So, Jillian; who are you running from, if you don't mind my asking? We're happy to take you on, but it's always good to know who we're sheltering."

Without hesitation, Jillian reached into her satchel and produced two large Aethyr Shards. They gleamed with radiant energy, their shimmering hues casting an ethereal glow in the early morning light. "These should be sufficient payment for my passage," she said. "As for who I'm running from; Zealots from Aldrosia. My homeland...isn't safe for me any more."

Ahlissa's eyes widened, taking in the shimmering shards with an almost reverent admiration. "Aethyr Shards. So, it's true; the Khystar do walk among us." Her expression softened as she returned the shards to Jillian's hands. "Rest assured, your presence here is safe with me and my crew. We'll take care of you."

Jillian's shoulders relaxed, a look of relief washing over her face. "Thank you, Ahlissa," she said quietly. "I've been on the run for a long time. I didn't realize how exhausted I was until now."

Ahlissa gave her shoulder a reassuring squeeze. "You're with us now. We're heading north soon, far from any reach of the Zealots. You'll have time to breathe and finally feel safe."

Aidan watched the exchange, feeling a wave of relief wash over him. Jillian was finally safe, and her presence on the Zephyr Breeze brought him a strange sense of solace he hadn't expected. With Ahlissa's protection and the vastness of the skies around them, he felt they had gained a small but meaningful advantage.

As the first rays of sunlight began to warm the deck, Aidan took a moment to soak in the view of Gideon City, watching as its spires and rooftops grew smaller and smaller beneath the ascending airship. He looked over at Jillian, who stood beside him, her face turned to the horizon with a calm he hadn't seen before.

"Looks like we're finally free," he murmured, half to himself.

Jillian nodded, her gaze unwavering. "For now, at least. I'd forgotten what freedom felt like." She turned to him, a faint smile tugging at the corners of her lips. "Thank you, Aidan. I don't think I could have done this alone."

"You're welcome. Besides," Aidan replied with a smile, "I'd say the adventure's just begun."

With a satisfied nod, Ahlissa gave the order to lift off. The crew, well-accustomed to her efficient style, sprang into action, casting off the last mooring ropes and setting the sails for the morning breeze. As the

Zephyr Breeze ascended, they left the looming presence of Gideon City far below, disappearing through wisps of mist and cloud.

17

The Machination

After ensuring that Tanith, a trusted crew member, would escort Jillian to the guest quarters, Ahlissa watched as Jillian, carrying only the essentials, disappeared down the stairway. "Thank you for accepting me," Jillian said to Ahlissa, with a brief nod to Aidan. "And thank you for trusting me."

Once Jillian was out of earshot, Ahlissa's gaze turned serious. "Aidan, come with me," she said, her voice calm but edged with an unspoken concern that Aidan couldn't ignore. He followed her to the airship's bridge, where she led him into a private, quiet chamber. The usually unflappable Ahlissa looked uncharacteristically pensive, a trait she rarely displayed. Aidan sensed immediately that something was weighing heavily on her mind.

"Take a seat," she instructed, gesturing to a plush chair. As they settled in, a silent crew member entered, placing a glass pitcher of chilled, fruit-flavoured water on the table and departed without a word, their demeanour as efficient as it was neutral.

Pouring a glass for each of them, Ahlissa handed one to Aidan before sitting across from him. "So," she began, her gaze fixed intently on him, "how did things go at the Broken Blade Inn last night? Aside from you bringing back Jillian, of course." Her voice was casual, but her eyes held a probing curiosity. "Anyone approach you? Try to pry for information about who you are?"

Aidan shook his head, meeting her gaze. "No one asked anything like that."

A hint of relief crossed Ahlissa's face, but her expression remained serious. "Good. But I need to tell you something," she said, lowering her voice. "Despite our efforts to remain unnoticed, your departure from the inn was... observed." She paused, her tone cautious but direct. "My associates informed me that The Observers - those men from last night - have taken a particular interest in you and Jillian. They're stationed at a nearby building by the Skybridge terminal, keeping a close watch on this airship."

Aidan frowned. "The Observers?"

Ahlissa nodded. "Yes. They're not ordinary thugs, Aidan. They report to The Seeker and The Gatherer. And, unfortunately, they're backed by The Sentinel. If things escalate, they have law enforcement at their disposal. I want to avoid unnecessary conflicts with Gideon's authority, but I think you should know that they're aware of Jillian's presence on board."

Aidan's face hardened. "Jillian is my responsibility. You don't know anything about her."

Ahlissa arched an eyebrow, a faint smile playing at her lips. "Oh, really? And what is it exactly that I 'don't know,' Aidan?"

"I mean, if anyone asks, you don't know," he clarified, with a half-hearted attempt at a grin.

Ahlissa chuckled, her eyes twinkling for a moment. "Ah, the art of selective ignorance. A useful tool in my line of work," she remarked with a wry smile, but her tone quickly grew sombre again. "What troubles me is how much influence The Observers have gained in such a short time. Did you notice anything unusual about them when you encountered them last night? Any visible weapons?"

Aidan shook his head again, recalling the unsettling encounter. "No weapons, but their eyes... they were black, like pools of ink."

Ahlissa's expression darkened. "Black eyes? That's... unusual, to put it lightly. They may be possessed or under some other form of malevolent influence. If they're hunting Jillian, they could very well be proxies for agents of the Aspiring Dream."

Aidan's brow furrowed as he absorbed the weight of her words. The Aspiring Dream was tied to whisperings of manipulation and darkness. "You think they're working for the Aspiring Dream?"

"Perhaps indirectly," Ahlissa said. "The Aspiring Dream operates through manipulation and control, often co-opting individuals to spread its influence. It's insidious. We've monitored the Observers for a while, but their main base lies within a compound on one of the floating islands above Gideon City. It's heavily guarded, and all our attempts to scry on it have been blocked. My suspicion is that The

Seeker aids them."

Aidan shook his head, his mind spinning. "It's hard to believe The Seeker would allow people like that to operate within the city."

Ahlissa leaned back, her fingers tapping lightly on the armrest. "Yet they do. And they're targeting Jillian. I understand she has an Aethyr Mark?"

Aidan nodded and pulled out the sketch Jillian had drawn of her mark. He handed it to Ahlissa, who studied it carefully, her expression shifting to one of intrigue.

"This mark... it's significant. If Jillian indeed has an Aethyr Mark, it explains why she's being hunted. The Zealots would never allow a mark to exist outside their control," Ahlissa mused. "Did she mention what kind of power her mark gives her?"

"No," Aidan admitted. "She hasn't fully explained it."

Ahlissa nodded thoughtfully, handing the sketch back. "This changes things, Aidan. The Observers will use any means necessary to reach her. You need to be prepared. They may attempt to infiltrate the ship or send an assassin."

Aidan felt a cold knot in his stomach as he absorbed her warning. "I'll stay on board. I won't do anything that could draw attention to her."

Ahlissa seemed reassured, and she leaned forward, her voice softening. "There's something else, Aidan, something I haven't shared before. You've probably wondered about my 'associates' and who they work for."

He nodded, his curiosity piqued.

She took a steadying breath. "I work for an organisation known as 'The Machination.' We answer to a group called 'The Glass Tower.' We're a covert network operating across Scylla, primarily made up of half-Aystar, though others are accepted as well. The Zephyr Breeze itself is part of this network, though to most it's just an airship. But our true mission is much larger than that. We call it 'The Prism.'"

Aidan processed this new information, finally understanding why Ahlissa always seemed to be a step ahead. "And you're not seeking control? You're not like the others?" he asked cautiously.

Ahlissa shook her head. "No. Our goal isn't to control Scylla, but to keep it balanced. We gather knowledge and intervene when necessary to prevent another devastating conflict like the Age of Calamity. We can't allow history to repeat itself."

Aidan nodded, feeling the gravity of her words. "I'll be careful. Jillian will be, too."

"Good," Ahlissa replied. "I'm sending a message to the Aystaran ambassador, briefing him on what we know about The Observers and their connections. We have to be careful, both politically and militarily."

Aidan stood, gratitude shining in his eyes. "Thank you, Ahlissa. For trusting me."

He left the chamber and made his way to Jillian's quarters. He knocked lightly, and when she opened the door, her face softened in relief.

"All settled in?" he asked.

Jillian nodded, glancing around the cosy room. "Yes, thank you. I finally feel... safe here."

Aidan leaned against the door frame, the weight of the morning's revelations fresh on his mind. "We're being watched, but we'll be leaving soon. We're headed somewhere... familiar but not quite home. You'll be safer there."

She studied him closely, her eyes filled with understanding. "You share their blood, but not their purpose. That's rare. I wonder why."

He looked away, feeling the familiar ache of old memories. "I was orphaned young, raised on Gideon's streets. Then I lived among the Aystar. I've never felt like I truly belonged anywhere; until this ship. It's the closest thing to a home I've ever had."

Jillian placed a gentle hand on his arm, her touch warm and grounding. "I'm sorry for what you've been through. But I can see you've found strength from it."

As they stood together in the quiet, Aidan realised he wasn't alone in his journey any more. Her touch calmed him and the tension across his shoulders eased.

"There's a darkness growing in Gideon City," Jillian continued. "I could feel it. The Observers were part of something much bigger. They're patient, methodical. The Aspiring Dream plays the long game, infiltrating societies and spreading its influence."

Aidan nodded. "Ahlissa thinks the same. She was already reaching out to the Aystaran ambassador to inform him of what's going on."

Jillian smiled. "That's a wise move. The Aystar are ancient and wise; they may be able to intervene before things escalate."

They spent the next hour together, sharing stories about their pasts, experiences, and the uncertain future ahead. Aidan introduced Jillian to some of the crew members and took her on a tour of the Zephyr Breeze. Jillian was fascinated by the ship's unique features, noting how different it was from other vessels she had seen.

"This ship feels special," she said, examining the lighting panels. "It doesn't run solely on elemental magic, does it?"

Aidan shrugged. "Honestly, I've never really thought about it. This is the only airship I've ever been on."

"It's impressive," Jillian said thoughtfully. "I'd love to study it more, if that's possible."

Aidan smiled. "I'm sure Ahlissa wouldn't mind."

18

Next Steps

As the Zephyr Breeze made its way to Sunhold, Aidan reflected on how much his life had changed in the past few days. Jillian's presence on the ship had added a new layer of intrigue, but also a sense of purpose. Together, they now had the potential to uncover deeper mysteries surrounding both the Kale Khestari and the Kale Ashtari.

The Kale Khestari at Sunhold viewed her with a mixture of curiosity and admiration; to most, she appeared as just another Aystar. But a few of the Keepers of the Past - the spiritual leaders of the Temple of Ages - seemed to recognise something deeper in her. They said nothing, but Jillian could tell they understood her true nature as a Khystar.

Throughout their stay, Jillian felt safe. The Kale Khestari, while strong-willed and fiercely independent, welcomed her presence. No one threatened her, and she sensed no other Khystar among them. However, Jillian remained determined to find others of her kind and unite them under the banner of her Aethyr Mark, so they could stand against the growing influence of the Aspiring Dream.

Over several days, Jillian and Aidan delved deeper into their respective quests. Jillian's determination to locate other Khystar grew stronger with each passing day. She often found herself standing on the highest walls of Sunhold, gazing into the horizon, lost in thoughts of the potential allies she hoped to find.

Meanwhile, Aidan became increasingly absorbed in his studies. He spent countless hours in the ship's modest library, poring over ancient manuscripts and translating texts that might hold the key to their mission. The discovery of the Dark Aethyr Shard had ignited a spark of hope and urgency within him. He frequently consulted with Jillian, sharing findings and discussing strategies.

"We'll need to be cautious," Jillian reminded him one evening, as they reviewed a particularly cryptic passage. "The Aldrosian Zealots are not to be underestimated, and their reach extends far beyond Gideon City."

Aidan nodded, his expression sombre. "I know. That's why we must tread carefully. If we can secure the support of Master Brevax and the Aystar ambassador, we might have a chance."

Jillian placed a reassuring hand on his arm. "We'll face these challenges together, Aidan. Remember, we have the strength of the Zephyr Breeze and its crew behind us."

With renewed determination, they finalised their plans. Aidan meticulously prepared the summary of his findings, ensuring it was comprehensive and persuasive. He and Ahlissa then coordinated their efforts, crafting a narrative that would appeal to The Thirteen and present their expedition as a noble quest for lost heritage.

Aidan spent many days scouring the ancient texts housed in Sunhold's libraries. His most recent find was both tantalizing and troubling. He had discovered an obscure cuneiform script, a blend of the ancient Aystar language and Argar, used during the height of the Argar Empire. The language was difficult to decipher, but Aidan's expertise in dark knowledge allowed him to make sense of it.

The text revealed the existence of a powerful Dark Aethyr Shard, an ancient relic that could hold immeasurable power. It had first been uncovered in the Forbidden Wastes by a monstrous Argar warlord named Drazakh Khan.

The shard was said to contain knowledge of a Kale Ashtari prophecy, a key sought after by the Keepers of the Past and their agents. But it had been lost when the Argar Empire fell, thousands of years ago, and its last known location was deep beneath Gideon City, in the ruins that now lay hidden beneath the metropolis.

This discovery could lead to something extraordinary; perhaps clues about the origins of humanity and other races in Scylla, or even a glimpse into the first language of the Kale Ashtari Prophecy. Yet, investigating such a find would require venturing into the Undercity, a perilous place controlled by various factions, and access was often forbidden. Aidan realised that to carry out this expedition, he would need permission from The Thirteen, Gideon City's ruling council.

Aidan considered his options. He needed someone reputable to front the expedition, someone The Thirteen would trust. His thoughts turned to Master Brevax, a scholar with influence in the city, but also someone Aidan was wary of due to his past ties. Even so, Master Brevax could be their way in. Deciding to consult Ahlissa about it, Aidan made his way through the winding streets of Sunhold to the bridge of the Zephyr Breeze.

When he found Ahlissa, she was overseeing the airship's navigation. She greeted him with a smile. "Aidan, you look troubled. What's on your mind?"

"I've found something," Aidan began. "There's a powerful Aethyr Shard hidden in the depths of Gideon City, possibly inscribed with the key to the first language of the Kale Ashtari Prophecy. It might even contain knowledge about the origins of all races in Scylla."

Ahlissa's eyebrows lifted with interest. "That's a bold claim. Tell me more. How do you plan to retrieve it?"

Aidan sighed. "We'd need to arrange an expedition into the Undercity. But with the Observers' influence here, convincing the council to grant us access will be difficult. They'll want the shard for themselves."

Ahlissa raised a hand, silencing him. "Leave that to me. Write a detailed summary of what you've uncovered, and I'll have my people craft a suitable cover story. We'll involve the Aystar ambassador to petition The Thirteen on our behalf, framing this as a search for a lost artefact important to the Aystar."

Aidan nodded and read out the full passage from the text he had deciphered, ensuring Ahlissa understood the significance of the find. She listened carefully, absorbing every detail.

"Thank you, Aidan," Ahlissa said once he finished. "Don't worry. We'll get this sorted. I'll arrange for either my own crew or some trusted diggers and explorers from my organisation to assist with the expedition."

"There's also Master Brevax," Aidan suggested. "He's still living here in Gideon, and he might be able to help us."

Ahlissa considered it. "Ah yes, Master Brevax. We were concerned about his possible ties to Lord Khannay and the Servants of Aroth, but nothing concrete has surfaced. He could be a valuable ally for this mission, especially since he's respected by The Thirteen. The Mhargrave Outreach Society monitors him, but we can run interference if needed."

Satisfied with their plan, Aidan set to work, writing a formal version of the text he had uncovered, including references to his sources for legitimacy. This document would be shared with the Aystar ambassador, who would use it to persuade the council to allow the expedition.

Three days later, everything was in place. Aidan informed Jillian of the upcoming expedition, and her curiosity was piqued.

"Do you want me to come with you?" she asked.

"That's up to you," Aidan replied.

Jillian smiled. "I'll join you. I can't hide forever, and I like helping my friends."

Aidan was glad to have her on board.

19

Air Power

On the final day of their stay in Sunhold, Ahlissa received a report that a large airship, dubbed Stormbringer, had been sighted twice in recent days amid unnatural storm activity. The captains of two other airships, the Zephyr Cloud and the Zephyr Spirit, confirmed the sightings.

The Zephyr Breeze began its journey back to Gideon City with two allied airships, the Zephyr Cloud and the Zephyr Spirit, gliding alongside it in a protective formation. Each ship, while unique in design, shared the same sleek, elegant lines characteristic of Ahlissa's fleet, making them both beautiful and imposing as they drifted through the skies. Their hulls gleamed in the sunlight, reinforced with layers of Aethyrite plating, shimmering subtly with iridescent hues. This material not only provided strong defensive properties but also enhanced the ships' agility, allowing them to respond swiftly to unexpected threats.

As the Zephyr Breeze took the lead, the Zephyr Cloud flew slightly above and to the right, maintaining a careful distance while mirroring the course precisely. The Zephyr Spirit kept to the rear, its positioning strategic, both to guard against possible ambushes from behind and to communicate with the Zephyr Breeze in case they encountered any turbulence or sighted the Stormbringer airship. Each vessel communicated through a series of signal lights and glyph flashes visible from a great distance, the glow of enchanted symbols lighting up as commands were issued and received. This silent, coordinated communication system allowed the three ships to remain in sync without drawing unnecessary attention from below.

In the cool, open air, the hum of the elemental rings that powered each airship filled the atmosphere, pulsing with a faint blue light as they carved through the sky. Aidan and Jillian stood on the deck of the Zephyr Breeze, observing the coordinated flight with fascination. From their vantage point, the Zephyr Cloud and Zephyr Spirit moved with uncanny precision, as if dancing to an unspoken rhythm in perfect harmony with the Zephyr Breeze.

The Zephyr Cloud was captained by Harvin, a seasoned Adeni sailor known for his sharp eye and unmatched instincts in evasive manoeuvres. Slightly smaller and faster than the Zephyr Breeze, it was often used as a scout or messenger. Onboard, Harvin and his crew constantly monitored the surrounding skies, scanning for any sign of the Stormbringer. They had been briefed on the unnatural storm sightings and knew to expect possible sudden weather changes. Harvin, standing at the bow with a spyglass in hand, kept his gaze trained on the horizon. The crew was on high alert, but their calm professionalism created a reassuring atmosphere on the deck.

The Zephyr Spirit, under the command of Captain Alira, was a formidable airship, carrying heavier weaponry than its counterparts. Unlike the smaller Zephyr Cloud, the Spirit boasted ballistae and mounted elemental cannons along its hull, ready to defend the fleet should an unexpected attack arise. The crew was a mix of seasoned soldiers and younger warriors eager to prove themselves. Alira herself was a skilled tactician, calm and calculating in times of tension. Her orders were concise and clear, the crew moving with practiced efficiency as they adjusted the sails and reinforced protective wards in case of potential combat.

Aidan found himself captivated by the coordination between the three airships. Each vessel operated as part of a cohesive unit, watching and protecting the other while maintaining the Breeze as the focal point of the formation. The display of trust between the captains and their crews demonstrated an underlying respect and loyalty among them. It was evident that they shared more than just a mission; they were bound by a mutual understanding of the dangers they could face in their line of work.

As the day turned into night, lanterns were lit on each airship, their golden glow illuminating the decks. The sight was both beautiful and surreal as the airships floated over the darkened landscape of Scylla, their lights like stars against the night sky. Ahlissa's crew maintained a steady pace and a sense of calm confidence, though Aidan noticed that many still cast wary glances into the vast shadows surrounding them.

Jillian leaned against the railing beside Aidan, glancing from ship to ship. "It's incredible to see them move in such unison," she said quietly, admiration in her voice. "You can tell they've worked together for years."

Aidan nodded, a faint smile on his lips. "There's a kind of unspoken language between them. They don't even need words to know what the other is doing. It's comforting to be part of a fleet like this."

Ahead of them, the distant lights of Gideon City began to twinkle on the horizon, signalling that the long voyage was drawing to a close as the three airships glided gracefully, side by side, back toward the familiar city skyline.

20

Beneath Gideon City

The city was alive with the anticipation of the Zephyr fleet's return; the sight of three vessels cutting through the clouds was a spectacle that hadn't graced the city's citizens in decades. The Zephyr Breeze, leading the Zephyr Cloud and Zephyr Spirit, descended slowly toward the main skybridge terminal, coming to rest in the designated docking bays where throngs of onlookers had gathered to witness their arrival.

Aidan, however, wasn't watching the descent in awe. He had been far too preoccupied with the tangle of questions that had been haunting him since their last encounter with the Observers, and now, he couldn't shake the feeling that the city held answers he had no choice but to pursue.

Once docked, he and Ahlissa stepped off the Zephyr Breeze, both intent on a briefing before he would go alone to the Northern Quarter to investigate a contact's report on his ancient Kale Ashtari bloodline. Ahlissa kept her tone sharp as she discussed the covert nature of their mission here, but her eyes kept wandering around the terminal. "Look, Aidan," she finally said, pulling him aside, "the whole city is in a state of quiet tension. That new fleet initiative launched by The Sentinel has everyone whispering, and now, these Observers... just keep your eyes open. Be discreet."

Aidan nodded, his mind elsewhere, just as a figure moved toward him from the shadows near the edge of the terminal. Aidan caught a flash of recognition in the man's smirk, a half-grin that held a dark amusement. It was Wayne Scarrow.

Scarrow, the relic hunter and former associate Aidan had tangled with back in Kanarzand, hadn't changed much. His wide-brimmed hat cast a shadow over his sharp, calculating eyes, and his movements were as confident as ever. He wore a well-tailored suit that seemed too stifling for the city's warm afternoon air, and he carried an air of intrigue and ill-intention about him. Scarrow sidled closer, hands casually in his pockets, as if they were old friends who happened to meet by chance.

"Aidan," he greeted, voice dripping with feigned warmth. "What a surprise. It's been some time, hasn't it?"

Aidan felt his muscles tighten instinctively, his mind flashing back to their last encounter in Kanarzand where Scarrow's so-called 'help' was effectively to threaten him. "Wayne," Aidan replied evenly, eyes locked on Scarrow's smirk. "What brings you to Gideon?"

"Oh, you know," Scarrow replied, with a light shrug. "Business. Research. The occasional ancient artefact that might just change the balance of power in our dear Scylla." His gaze flicked over Aidan's shoulder toward the Zephyr Breeze. "Quite a fleet you've got there. I didn't know you travelled in such esteemed company now."

Aidan held his ground. "It's hardly the most pressing thing happening in Gideon City right now. But you already know that don't you?"

Scarrow's smirk widened, his eyes glinting with a mixture of admiration and challenge. "You catch on quickly, Aidan. Yes, I do know a few things." He stepped in closer, lowering his voice. "I happen to know the Observers are particularly interested in you. And your... companion from Aldrosia."

Aidan didn't flinch, though the mention of Jillian confirmed that Scarrow's motives were far from friendly. He crossed his arms and met Scarrow's gaze, silently waiting.

"Look," Scarrow said, dropping the playfulness, "I know you're the cautious type. You wouldn't be getting mixed up with the Observers or hiding an Aethyr Marked Khystar without good reason. But you're diving head first into something dangerous here, Aidan. They've been following you and that girl since you arrived."

"Why the sudden interest in my affairs, Scarrow?" Aidan asked, arching an eyebrow. "I don't remember us ever being on the same side."

"We're not," Scarrow replied easily, though his voice held a faint edge. "But I know an opportunity when I see one, and you're part of it. You could use someone with my... experience. That is, unless you plan to handle the Observers and every other threat on your own."

Aidan suppressed a scoff. "I think I'll manage."

"Ah, but you're not the only one they're watching," Scarrow countered smoothly. "In fact, I recently heard something interesting about the

Aethyr Shards you've been protecting. The ones hidden on that little ship of yours. Quite the precious cargo, wouldn't you say?"

Aidan's face hardened, but he held his composure. "I have no idea what you're talking about."

Scarrow gave a low chuckle, obviously enjoying this. "Please, Aidan. Give me a little more credit. I know about the shards, and I know exactly why they're valuable. You think I just happened to cross paths with you here?"

Aidan felt his pulse quicken as he tried to gauge Scarrow's angle. Scarrow was slippery, with a reputation for deception and manipulation, and his motives were always layered beneath his clever words.

"Alright, Wayne," Aidan said, keeping his tone carefully measured, "let's cut to it. What do you want?"

Scarrow's expression changed, his gaze becoming more intense. "A partnership, of sorts. I want in on whatever it is you're after with these shards. And I think you could use my help dealing with the Observers. There's more to them than you realise. They're not just tracking Jillian because she's Khystar. They're hunting for something much bigger; something that ties to the ancient powers in Scylla, powers that those in your bloodline might have once possessed."

Aidan hesitated, his mind racing. Scarrow's words hit close to the mark, and he wondered just how much the man truly knew about the Kale Ashtari or his connection to them. "Why would I ever trust you?" Aidan finally asked, not breaking eye contact.

"Trust?" Scarrow gave a short laugh. "Who said anything about trust? I'm just offering a mutually beneficial arrangement. I help you navigate the seedy underbelly of Gideon City, get you some insider intel on the Observers and their intentions, maybe even buy you some time to find what you're looking for without interference. And in return, you keep me informed on the Aethyr Shards' progress and anything you uncover in your little history hunt."

Aidan stared at him, his face an unreadable mask. "And what makes you think I'm after history? Or that I even care to share any of it with you?"

Scarrow held up his hands, palms out. "Aidan, please. You've always had that fire, that need to know. Ever since Kanarzand. It's why you're still alive, after all."

There was an awkward silence, both men holding their positions, neither willing to make the first move. Aidan found himself analysing Scarrow's face, searching for any indication that this was more than just a game to him. But there was no telling with Scarrow; he was all guile and cunning, an expert in the art of the double-cross.

"What's the catch?" Aidan finally asked, crossing his arms tightly.

Scarrow's grin returned, cold and calculating. "Simple: if, at any point, you decide my services are no longer worth it, I walk. But know this: I'll take what I know about you, about Jillian, about the Aethyr Shards, straight to The Gatherer or The Seeker, and I guarantee they'll be very interested in hearing about what's on that ship."

Aidan felt a surge of anger but fought to contain it. Scarrow was always a master manipulator, and this was no different. If he pushed him away, he risked giving Scarrow a reason to act out of spite. But accepting his help meant potentially inviting betrayal into his plans.

"You've changed a bit since Kanarzand," Aidan said slowly, a slight edge to his voice. "But not enough to hide what you really are. You're just here to make a profit, to gain something from this."

Scarrow shrugged, unperturbed. "Maybe so. But unlike others, I'm being upfront about it. I'm offering a bargain you can accept or refuse. Take it or leave it."

Aidan weighed his options, his mind racing. He could ignore Scarrow, continue as planned, and hope that he and Jillian could evade The Observers on their own. But Scarrow's knowledge of the city's underground was invaluable, and there was no denying he had contacts that could open doors Aidan might not even know existed.

And if Scarrow's information was accurate, the threat from the Observers was even greater than he had anticipated. Aidan had to admit, despite his misgivings, that Scarrow's offer was tempting.

"Fine," Aidan said at last, the words sounding bitter in his mouth. "I'll accept your... assistance. But only if you follow my terms."

Scarrow's grin widened. "I knew you'd come around. So, what's the plan?"

Aidan narrowed his eyes. "First, you'll stay away from Jillian. She has no part in whatever agreement we're making. You deal only with me. Understood?"

Scarrow gave an exaggerated nod, his eyes gleaming with amusement. "Understood."

"Second, you give me everything you know about The Observers, including their weaknesses, connections, and any contacts they have in the city."

"Of course. I'll even throw in a few pointers for moving about unnoticed in Gideon's shadier circles." Scarrow's tone was light, almost mocking, as if the whole arrangement was merely a diversion to him.

"Lastly," Aidan said, his voice low and steady, "if I even suspect you're holding back or misleading me, we're done. And you know just how much I'm willing to do to keep Jillian and the Aethyr Shards safe."

Scarrow met his gaze, his smile faltering for the briefest moment. "Understood," he replied, his voice softer, though a glint of mischief still lingered in his eyes.

Aidan studied him for a long moment before nodding. "Good. Then you can start by telling me what the Observers are really after."

Scarrow's grin returned, sly and knowing. "Gladly." He leaned in, his voice dropping to a conspiratorial whisper. "They're after power, Aidan. The kind of power that doesn't just make men wealthy but makes them gods. And if you're not careful, they'll stop at nothing to claim it."

Aidan felt a chill run through him, though he forced himself to keep his expression neutral. He had known, in some way, that this was bigger than just the shards or Jillian's mark. But hearing it confirmed sent a fresh wave of dread through him.

"Then I guess it's a good thing you're here," Aidan said quietly.

Scarrow gave him a mocking salute. "Count on it," he said menacingly and stalked away into the crowd.

The rest of the crew disembarked with a mix of relief and readiness, and Jillian was among them. She could see Aidan at the side of the docking station platform, engaged in an animated discussion with a tall man that she immediately recognised. She waited until the man departed and approached Aidan.

"Are you OK?" she asked.

"I think so," Aidan replied. "Unfortunately, I have a habit of running into old rivals in this place."

"Was that Wayne Scarrow," Jillian enquired. "Is he after something from you, again?"

"I've warned him to leave us alone," Aidan told her. "He tells me he knows about our Aethyr Marks; he has threatened to go to The Seeker and The Gatherer about us and he also claims to know about Ahlissa's smuggling operations."

"I see, what does he want from us, to secure his silence?"

"He wants me to tell him about our discoveries in return for his help to evade The Observers and to navigate the less desirable parts of the city."

"Then we will feed him enough detail to keep him interested and distracted," she told Aidan reassuringly. "Don't worry. He's all ego and bluster. It's best we get moving."

Aidan and Jillian, after exchanging a few words with their fellow crew members, made their way through the bustling streets toward the meeting point. The city's vibrancy at night was a stark contrast to the serene flight they had just experienced, with lanterns illuminating the pathways and the hum of conversation filling the air.

When they reached the rendezvous point beneath the grand archways of Gideon City, the expedition team was assembled, consisting of diggers funded by the Aystaran Embassy, explorers and specialists provided by Cordovar University, mercenaries from The Machination, crew members from the Zephyr Breeze, Master Brevax - representing The Thirteen – and, of course, Jillian and Aidan themselves.

As anticipated, The Thirteen agreed to grant access to the Undercity but were curious about the true nature of the expedition. They asked probing questions; What was the artefact's significance? Who else knew about it? What would Aidan do with the discovery once it was retrieved? Ahlissa skilfully deflected their concerns, emphasizing that the mission was under the purview of the Aystar and their embassy.

Yet there was another obstacle. The self-styled Queen of the Old Argar portion of the Undercity - a powerful figure who controlled access to the deeper ruins - needed to be appeased. It was customary to offer her a gift to ensure safe passage. Aidan sought permission to use the crystal the Aystar ambassador had once given him, and permission was granted.

Preparations were finalised, but Aidan remained uneasy. He knew

The Observers were watching. Jillian, sensitive to their presence, took measures to conceal both of them as they disembarked the Zephyr Breeze, casting enhanced spells to render them invisible. Aidan also disguised himself as best he could.

"The Observers are here," Jillian whispered. "I can feel them. They've seen the airship return."

Before they left, Ahlissa handed Aidan a small silver rod, inscribed with Aystar runes. "This is a gift from the ambassador," she explained. "Speak the command word – '*Obfuscate*' – and it will prevent scrying for twelve hours within a wide radius."

Aidan and Jillian joined the rest of the team at a safe location in the city, a small building where they could prepare without drawing attention. The team gathered in a meeting chamber, where Master Brevax greeted Aidan with open arms.

"Young Master Aidan!" Brevax exclaimed. "What a pleasant surprise. I didn't expect to see you on this expedition. It's a small world, isn't it?"

"I'm just here to help decipher some ancient writing," Aidan said with a smile.

"Yes, I hear we're searching for a fascinating artefact; a device inscribed with ancient symbols. It may shed light on the origins of the Aystar in this region."

"Exactly. I found something similar in a ruined city, which led me to believe this artefact might be connected."

Brevax nodded approvingly. "Very good. Now, let's get started. Do we have the gift for Queen Ashkaan ready?"

Aidan produced the crystal, and Brevax inspected it carefully. "Exquisite," Brevax said. "She'll be pleased."

Before they set out, Brevax gave the team a quick briefing. "Not all parts of the Undercity are stable or safe. There are vermin, traps, and worse lurking in the depths. The Sentinel occasionally sends teams to clear out the most dangerous areas, but many threats remain. Stay alert."

The team split into small groups and travelled separately to avoid attracting attention. They arrived at the Old Quarter without incident, finding the entrance to the tunnels hidden in the basement of a long-abandoned building.

As they descended into the dark, rough-hewn tunnels of the Undercity, they were met by two hulking Agar. They both glared at the group, their massive hands gripping crude weapons.

"State your business," one of them growled.

Master Brevax stepped forward calmly. "We seek an audience with Queen Ashkaan. We bring her a gift and request safe passage."

The second Argar grunted, while the first one seemed to consider the request. "Follow," he finally said.

The group followed the Argar through winding tunnels until they reached a wider chamber. The walls were adorned with fine tapestries, and luxurious carpets lined the floor; an odd juxtaposition to the rough surroundings.

At the centre of the chamber, lounging on a large, ornate couch, was Queen Ashkaan, known as a figure of menace and mystery; her very presence filled the underground hall with a bone-chilling air. An intricately crafted metal helmet covered her face and eyes completely, a dark, spiked visage with a sinister design, forged with jagged patterns and moulded to fit her head seamlessly, projected a nightmarish, almost otherworldly appearance.

She stretched lazily and regarded the group with mild curiosity. "Why do you disturb me?" she demanded.

Master Brevax bowed deeply. "Your majesty, we seek passage into the deeper ruins. We have come to pay our respects and offer this gift in exchange for your favour."

He presented the crystal, which Queen Ashkaan inspected with interest. "It is magical," she mused. "A fine gift. You have my permission to explore the depths but know this: cause no harm to my people, or you will not leave alive."

She leaned back and added, "You are not the first to pass this way recently. A team from Sindarr, sponsored by a man named Mhorvaeus, and protected by soldiers from the Jade Talon, has already gone into the depths. They, too, seek something. You may meet them down there."

With the queen's blessing, the two hulking Argar guards led the group to a large, rusted iron grate that blocked the entrance to an ancient tunnel. Beyond it lay a steep descent into the dark unknown. The real journey was about to begin, but Aidan couldn't shake the feeling that Mhorvaeus' team were already ahead of them, pursuing the same prize.

21

A Servant of Aroth Revealed

With a grunt, the two Argar left Aidan and his companions, saying, "Wait here if you return." Master Brevax led the group through the gap beneath the rusted iron portcullis, lighting their way with spells and magical items as they navigated a labyrinth of natural and humanoid-carved tunnels. Occasional caverns opened up, some empty and others filled with debris that had fallen from above.

The air was warm and humid, with a gentle airflow, and the porous rock walls seemed to "breathe." After three hours of exploration, they found a clear downward path. The lead mercenary called back, "I see stone steps leading to a large cavern."

"We move forward," Master Brevax instructed. The group cautiously descended the well-preserved steps into an ancient stone plaza, surrounded by ruined buildings. The mercenaries were on edge, glancing around at the skeletal remains and broken weapons littering the area.

"There are many skeletons here," the priest Zenot noted. "Some Argar. Others, possibly Aystar," added one of the specialists.

Master Brevax confirmed, "This area dates back to the Age of Calamity when the Argar Empire clashed with the Kale Khestari."

Ahlissa's crew exchanged glances, proud of their heritage. Jillian turned to Aidan and asked, "Your ancestors were warriors too. Does this history stir pride or sadness?"

Aidan replied quietly, "Sadness. We'll never know who they were or why they fought."

Jillian, offering comfort, placed a hand on his shoulder. "It's never easy to see such loss, especially when it's connected to your own people."

A mercenary interrupted, pointing to the ground. "Recent tracks. Perhaps two days old. A large group moved through here, heading toward those buildings."

"Could it be Mhorvaeus' group?" Master Brevax asked.

"Possibly, but we can't be sure," Zenot warned. "We should stay alert."

Master Brevax turned to the priest. "What can you sense?"

The priest clutched his holy symbol, eyes closed as he chanted, and then he spoke: "I see a large force, heavily armed, led by an aristocrat bearing the mark of the Jade Talon. They seek what we seek and will stop at nothing."

Master Brevax grimly nodded. "As I feared. Prepare for trouble. The Jade Talon's warriors are fanatical and dangerous. Stay close, Aidan."

Aidan suggested they may be following two groups. "If these tracks are only two days old, why did it take them five days to get here? Maybe they were searching elsewhere or got lost."

Master Brevax agreed. "We'll rest here while the mercenaries check for any older tracks." They set up camp in a large, ruined building, with Ahlissa's crew standing guard. The mercenaries split up, two heading back to search for additional tracks, while three scouts moved ahead.

After two hours, the rear scouts returned with nothing new to report; no other tracks. "They likely concealed their trail," one mercenary said. "We found some caverns that showed signs of digging, but nothing appeared to have been removed."

The lead scouts returned later, reporting a large stone bridge ahead leading into a cavern filled with debris. "We followed the tunnels beyond that, and there are sounds of digging and bright lights up ahead. They've definitely found something, but there are guards posted."

Master Brevax frowned, deep in thought. "Did you see any markings?"

"Yes," Zenot replied. "They are servants of the Jade Talon."

"Negotiating with them is pointless," Aidan said. "They won't listen."

"I agree," Brevax responded. "They're too committed to their cause. We've come too far to turn back now. We'll need magic and precision to overcome their numbers. Zenot, what did you see of their leader?"

Zenot shrugged. "A tall man in fine robes. Pale. He was supervising the dig."

Aidan immediately suggested it might be Lord Khannay, a vampire thought to be dead. Brevax was shocked but sceptical. "If it is him, we'll need to be prepared for a vampire. Are we ready?" He turned to the priests.

"We have holy water and daylight spells," Demetrius confirmed. The others nodded, ready with magical fire to disrupt the enemy camp.

Zenot outlined the situation. "They've got four soldiers on watch and about twenty more scattered. They're also using slaves to dig, with a few sorcerers and a dark priest for magical support."

They formed a plan. The mercenaries and Ahlissa's crew would take out the soldiers, while the specialists and Aidan focused on the spellcasters. Jillian and the diggers were kept out of the fighting.

After resting and preparing, the group moved out. They crossed an ancient stone bridge and followed the tunnels until they saw the pale magical light and heard the sounds of digging. The air was tense as they approached.

The mercenaries quickly and silently eliminated the four guards with arrows. The rest of the enemy camp was still unaware, too focused on their dig. Aidan led the next strike, suggesting flying and invisibility spells to approach the sorcerers.

The group attacked swiftly. Fireballs exploded near the dark altar, sending spellcasters and their leader flying. Aidan unleashed Velis' rod, channelling chain lightning that tore through the dark priest, sorcerers, and several Jade Talon soldiers. The cavern filled with chaos; fire, lightning, and brilliant daylight spells blinding the enemy.

Aidan swooped down, beheading the incapacitated sorcerer while the mercenaries and crew finished off the soldiers. The dark priest lay dead, his face melted. Aidan, suspecting the priest might rise again, severed his head as a precaution.

Amidst the carnage, the leader, trapped in a shimmering energy sphere, cursed loudly. "Do you know who you're dealing with? Release me! I'm here on official business, backed by powerful allies."

Master Brevax, ensuring his people were unharmed, turned to the trapped man. "Then name yourself good Sir; state your allegiance and your business beneath Gideon City."

The man curses and then says "I am Baron Von-Claagen, of the Sindarr Nation and you will release me at once. I am on a sponsored expedition and until you interfered by attacking us without provocation, we had nearly completed our business. What manner of dog are you, to think you have the right to attack and steal our findings?"

Master Brevax looked at Aidan and says "What do you think we do with him? He hasn't quite claimed diplomatic immunity, but he seems to have a position of power in a neighbouring state. Or least he claims so by indicating his title."

Aidan looked back at Brevax and says "Truly, I do not care what his status is. He is evil and should be destroyed."

Brevax nodded and then turned to the trapped man. "We have reason to believe that your exploration is in fact, illegal and that you are in league with dark forces. The evidence is clear. You had a priest of the Dark Religion in your company, and we have reason to suspect you as a vampire. Prove otherwise and you may yet live to see a cell in the Military Quarter of this fine city that you stain with your presence."

The pale man is angered by this and says "Tread carefully, old man, for my allies are very powerful and you would well to heed this as a final warning. I am not a vampire ..."

Aidan studies the man's appearance and can see unmistakable traits as though the man were a vampire. He is pale and he has sunken features; there is no life in his eyes, which are dark. But he does not have clawed hands and his teeth are normal, despite his rage.

"... I am a member of a noble house of Sindarr. If something happens to me then war will be the result. The mighty legions of Sindarr will once again rise and take the battlefield and Gideon City would cease to be what it is. Are you willing to risk the freedom of so many people by inviting such a declaration of war? Avoid it. Let me go."

"No," Aidan tells him and approaches.

Brevax looks horrified and says "What are you doing? We may have a diplomatic incident on our hands?"

"Who knows he is down here? A rock might have fallen on him ... who would know? Who would truly care? Diplomatic incident ... no, I disagree. As for your features, Baron, although you might look like the living, I have seen your features before ... so yes, I believe you are a vampire. With the fact you are in the company of people we would rather see dead than walking the streets of Gideon and since you were treating your diggers like slaves ... I don't see why we should be wasting time talking time to you, for in that pit is something we have come to claim, and we have a greater right to do so than you."

The man seething and cursing with rage, barely able to contain himself. Brevax looks to his priests, and they pray and cast divinations to further assess his true nature; "He is evil but is not undead" they say.

"Aidan ... he cannot be a vampire, the gods themselves have not revealed that."

"Then he is something else. An aberration perhaps. I have seen enough, Master Brevax, to know that he is not one of us. We must either continue this discussion or destroy him; I say destroy him."

"Then it saddens me that we undertake such a course of action," Brevax says. "Yet it is reasonable. You sir, Baron as you may claim to be, offer us no proof nor convincing evidence. Only threats. Threats of war and threats against our own lives. Had you been reasonable and willing to listen, then perhaps we may have let you go. But it is too late for that. You are evil and I know for a fact that you have no business being here. You have no official petition or documents signed by The Thirteen. I am their able representative and beneath Gideon City there is no true law that applies, save that imposed by The Thirteen's representatives. I hereby sanction your execution upon suspicion that you are a declared enemy of this state. Once the sphere that traps you is diminished, you will be put to death by magical fire. Have you anything further to say that might stay our hands?"

The Baron simply regards everyone coldly and he says, "Then so be it." Then he turns specifically to Aidan and speaks in a voice that sounds like a thousand whispers carried by the wind ... Aidan recognises the unmistakable language of the undead ... and Baron Von-Claagen tells him "There is one who will claim you and your time is short. He already knows you." Then he turns back to Master Brevax ... "do your worst, old man, enjoy the prize you have taken from me. May it be your undoing."

Then he stands there and awaits his fate, glaring at them silently and with hatred.

The sorcerer drops the sphere, and he is annihilated with magical fire. He screams and is incinerated easily, leaving nothing but ash where he stood. The priests cast further divinations and confirm that Baron Von-Claagen is dead. He has not escaped.

"I hope this was worth the effort, Aidan," Master Brevax says. He gestures to the side of the cavern where the dig was in progress. The expedition's diggers resumed their work where the other slaves had fled.

As the Baron's charred remains settled into ash, a heavy silence filled the cavern. The firelight from the magical flames flickered against the rock walls, casting long, eerie shadows. Aidan stood still, breathing heavily, still replaying the Baron's last words in his mind: *"There is one who will claim you, and your time is short. He already knows you."*

22

The Shard of Drazakh Khan

Master Brevax finally broke the silence. "Well, it is done. We have eliminated a potential threat, though I wish it had not come to this. The Baron was clearly a dangerous figure, but I cannot help but feel uneasy about his final words."

Aidan nodded, his thoughts racing. There was a chill in the Baron's voice when he spoke those final words, a promise of something sinister lurking in the shadows of his future. But now was not the time to dwell on it. The mission at hand still demanded his attention.

Jillian stepped forward, her face betraying a hint of concern. "Aidan, are you all, right? That man...whatever he was, seemed to know something about you."

"I'm fine," Aidan said, brushing off her concern. "But there's no time to waste. We need to see what they were digging for."

Master Brevax gestured toward the excavation site on the far side of the cavern. "Indeed. Let us hope the artefact remains intact. We've come too far to turn back empty-handed."

The group made their way cautiously toward the dig site. The twenty slaves who had once been under the Baron's control now cowered in the shadows, watching with wary eyes but making no move to flee. The remains of their tools - picks and shovels - lay scattered around the large pit, which descended steeply into the ground.

Zenot, the priest, stepped forward and knelt at the edge of the pit, examining the recently disturbed earth. "They were digging deep. Whatever they were after is close."

Ahlissa's crew and the mercenaries quickly organized, descending into the pit with the diggers they brought along. The specialists from Cordovar University followed close behind, eager to uncover the artefact buried beneath layers of history. Aidan, Jillian, and Master Brevax remained at the edge, overseeing the process.

Hours passed as the diggers carefully cleared away rubble and debris. The air in the cavern grew thick with tension as everyone sensed they were drawing closer to something significant. Finally, one of the diggers called out, his voice echoing off the stone walls.

"I've found something! There's something here!"

The diggers moved with renewed energy, shifting rocks and dirt until, at last, the object of their search was revealed. Buried beneath centuries of earth and stone was a massive Aethyr Shard. It was unlike anything Aidan had ever seen; a translucent black crystal, easily the size of a man's torso, pulsing faintly with an eerie, dark amber glow.

"It's beautiful…" Jillian whispered, her eyes wide with awe.

Master Brevax stepped closer, his eyes narrowing as he examined the shard from a distance. "This…this is it. The shard described in the ancient texts. A relic of incredible power."

Aidan, still wary, approached the shard with caution. As he drew nearer, he felt a faint, unsettling hum in the air, as if the shard itself was alive, vibrating with ancient energy. He had read about Aethyr Shards before; fragments of Aethyr, infused with immense magical potential. But this one felt different. Older. Darker.

"Be careful," Aidan warned. "We don't know what kind of magic this shard holds."

Master Brevax nodded. "Indeed. We must handle it with the utmost caution. Its power could be beyond anything we've encountered."

As they continued to examine the shard, Jillian tilted her head, as if listening to something the others couldn't hear. "There's something… off about it. It's like it's…calling out to something."

Aidan looked at her sharply. "What do you mean?"

"I don't know," she said, frowning. "It's like it's trying to communicate. But not with us. With something else."

Before Aidan could respond, Zenot suddenly shouted from the other side of the pit. "We've got company!"

23

The Jade Talon

The group turned to see several figures emerging from the shadows of the cavern's entrance. They were heavily armoured, wearing dark cloaks and helmets that concealed their faces. And emblazoned on their armour was the unmistakable symbol of the Jade Talon.

"How did they find us?" Aidan muttered under his breath, drawing his weapon.

Master Brevax frowned, his brow furrowed in concern. "I feared they might send reinforcements. Prepare yourselves. This will not be an easy fight."

Aidan tightened his grip on his sword. "Jillian, stay close to me. We can't afford to let them get the shard."

Jillian nodded, her expression tense. She reached for the magical focus hanging from her belt, ready to cast at a moment's notice.

The Jade Talon soldiers advanced swiftly, their leader - a towering figure in heavy black armour - barking orders as they moved into formation. There was at least a dozen of them, heavily armed and moving with precision.

"They're too organized," Aidan whispered. "They've been tracking us."

"Hold the line!" Zenot called out to his mercenaries, positioning them to block the enemy's advance. Ahlissa's crew moved into defensive positions, readying their crossbows and magical weapons.

The first wave of Jade Talon soldiers charged forward, their swords gleaming in the dim light. Aidan raised his blade, meeting their attack with swift, practiced movements. Steel clashed against steel, the sound echoing in the cavern as the battle erupted.

Jillian, standing just behind Aidan, unleashed a barrage of magical energy, sending bolts of force toward the advancing soldiers. Each hit struck with precision, knocking the attackers off balance. But for every soldier that fell, more seemed to take their place.

"They're not letting up!" Jillian shouted over the noise of the battle.

Aidan parried a strike from one of the soldiers, countering with a quick slash that sent the man stumbling back. "We need to protect the shard! If they get their hands on it, we're done for."

Master Brevax, standing near the shard, called out incantations, summoning a protective barrier around the crystal. A shimmering dome of arcane energy formed, shielding the shard from harm; for the time being.

The leader of the Jade Talon forces, his dark armour gleaming in the pale light, stepped forward. His voice boomed across the battlefield, commanding his troops with unwavering authority.

"The shard belongs to us! Surrender it, and your deaths will be swift. Resist, and you will suffer!"

Aidan glared at the man. "You'll have to take it from us first."

The leader's eyes narrowed behind his helmet, and with a snarl, he raised his blade and charged directly toward Aidan.

The two clashed in a fury of strikes and parries, their swords ringing out with each blow. Aidan fought with everything he had, but the Jade Talon leader was relentless, his strength and speed far greater than Aidan had anticipated.

Jillian, seeing Aidan struggle, raised her hands and chanted a spell, sending a burst of fire toward the leader. The flames licked at his armour, but he shrugged it off, barely slowed.

"Is that the best you can do?" the leader sneered, swinging his blade with brutal force. Aidan barely managed to block the strike, but the impact sent him staggering back.

As the battle raged on, it became clear that the Jade Talon had the upper hand. Their numbers, combined with their ferocity, were beginning to overwhelm Aidan's group.

"We can't hold them off much longer!" Zenot shouted, fending off two soldiers at once.

Master Brevax, his face pale with exertion, called out from behind the protective barrier around the shard. "We must retreat! We can't let them have the shard, but we can't win this fight either!"

Aidan knew he was right. They were outnumbered, and the Jade Talon showed no signs of retreating. but how could they escape with the shard?

Amidst the thunderous clash of steel and the cries of battle, Aidan's heart pounded like a war drum. He parried a blow from another soldier and glanced around, taking in the chaotic scene. Jillian's flames roared, casting a flickering light over the cavern, while Ahlissa and Master Brevax fought side by side, their skills and magic forming a formidable defence.

Aidan's eyes locked onto the Aethyr Shard, the object of their struggle. The ancient artefact gleamed with an otherworldly light, its importance evident in the way the Jade Talon soldiers threw themselves at the defenders, desperate to seize it.

"Fall back to the shard!" Aidan commanded, his voice cutting through the din. "We need to make our stand there!"

Zenot and the others responded instantly, closing ranks around the precious relic. The air was thick with the scent of sweat and blood, and the ground was littered with the fallen. Aidan could see the strain on his comrades' faces, the weariness in their eyes, but there was no room for retreat in their hearts.

Suddenly, a resounding horn echoed through the cavern. From the shadows emerged the agents of the New Kanarzand Bureau of Forbidden

Archaeology, their dark cloaks swirling as they descended upon the battlefield. Led by their enigmatic mistress, Sainar, they moved with deadly precision, their weapons flashing in the low light.

"For the Bureau!" Mistress Sainar's voice rang out, cold and commanding. Her presence was like a beacon to the beleaguered defenders, infusing them with renewed strength.

The Jade Talon soldiers faltered, momentarily taken aback by the sudden reinforcements. Ahlissa took advantage of the distraction, her blade dancing as she carved a path through the enemy ranks. Master Brevax's magic flared, creating barriers and hurling arcane blasts that sent soldiers flying.

"We've got your back!" shouted one of Sainar's agents to Aidan, covering him with well-aimed crossbow bolts. "Focus on the shard!"

Aidan nodded, his resolve hardening. He fought his way to Jillian, who was still beside the shard, her chanting growing more fervent. "Almost there!" she yelled over the noise, her voice strained with the effort of maintaining the spell.

The enemy leader, a hulking figure in dark armour, roared in fury and charged once more. But this time, Sainar herself intercepted him, her twin blades a blur of lethal grace. "You will not have it!" she hissed, matching his strength with her skill.

The battle raged, and the defenders held their ground, inch by inch. The agents of the Bureau wove through the chaos, their precise strikes and spells bolstering the group's defences. Slowly, the tide began to turn.

The defenders pushed back with newfound vigour. Sainar's lethal dance continued to hold the enemy leader at bay, her movements fluid and unyielding. The agents of the Bureau struck down the remaining Jade Talon soldiers with unwavering precision, their dark cloaks billowing like shadows in the tumultuous clash.

With a final, desperate roar, the enemy leader fell to his knees, defeated by Sainar's relentless assault. "Retreat!" came a frantic cry from the remaining Jade Talon forces, scattering into the darkness from whence they came.

As the dust settled, Aidan rushed to Mistress Sainar, his breath heavy yet filled with gratitude. "Mistress Sainar," he said, bowing his head slightly, "we owe you, our lives. Your timely intervention has turned the tide of this battle."

Sainar sheathed her twin blades, a slight smile playing on her lips. "The Bureau is committed to preserving history, not letting it fall into the wrong hands," she replied. "We are allies in this endeavour."

Aidan glanced at his exhausted companions, then back to Sainar. "We must leave the Undercity swiftly with the shard. The Queen's spies will certainly be alerted by now."

"Indeed," Sainar agreed. She signalled to one of her agents, who stepped forward. "Show them the concealed path through the lower tunnels. It will lead you to a hidden exit far from the eyes of Queen Ashkaan's minions."

The agent nodded and motioned for Aidan and his companions to follow. "Thank you," Aidan said, his voice filled with earnest appreciation.

"Your aid has secured our escape."

"Go quickly," Sainar urged. "And be vigilant. The path is treacherous, but it is your best chance to evade pursuit."

With one last look at the battlefield and a nod of farewell to their saviours, Aidan and his companions followed the agent, disappearing into the shadows of the hidden passage. Their mission was far from over, but for now, they had a fighting chance to secure the Aethyr Shard and uncover its secrets without the immediate threat of Queen Ashkaan's forces.

24

Securing the Dark Aethyr Shard

When they returned to the surface, Aidan and his expedition team found that it was dusk. As the light faded, the companions found themselves on the fringes of New Kanarzand. They had escaped from the dangerous Undercity.

Jillian collapsed to her knees, exhausted from the effort of the battle and using magic. Aidan knelt beside her, placing a hand on her shoulder.

"We did it," he said, his voice filled with relief.

Jillian smiled weakly. "Yes, but this isn't over. The Jade Talon will come for the shard again."

"And, if it is not them then other groups will come after it," Ahlissa warned. "The Silent Crescent and The Sceptre Guilds would also seek to control its power."

Master Brevax approached, his face grave. "Indeed. We've bought ourselves time, but not much. We need to secure the shard, and quickly.

The knowledge it holds could change everything."

Aidan looked at the shard. Its dark glow seemed to pulse with an even greater intensity than before, as if aware of the chaos it had caused. He could see runes forming and vanishing within it as it changed.

"We'll find a way," Aidan said, determination in his voice. "But for now, we need to regroup and prepare for what's coming. This artefact needs to be hidden and studied."

"The Ambassador is expecting us," Ahlissa informed them and cast a firm glance at Aidan. "I have made advance arrangements with our Embassy for an urgent diplomatic consignment to be secured."

Master Brevax and Jillian nodded in agreement.

Master Brevax pulled Aidan aside. "I've risked a lot for you," he said. "I'll inform The Thirteen that we retrieved the artefact and fought off Jade Talon's servants in the Undercity, including their leader and a Sindarr noble. I'll warn them about possible repercussions, though war is unlikely. Others may still come looking."

Aidan nodded. "I appreciate your help. I realize the situation with Baron Von-Claagen was intense. Perhaps I should have handled it with more diplomacy."

Ahlissa joined them, her expression thoughtful. "Diplomacy is often a luxury we don't have in the field. Your decision was necessary, Aidan."

"I understand your concerns," Brevax replies. "But I don't intend to inform The Thirteen about our suspicions regarding the bloodline of

Aroth. The Baron may have looked vampiric, but our priest couldn't confirm he was undead. We can't be certain of his nature, just that he served dark powers. Speculation on Aroth's bloodline influencing events here is premature."

Aidan warns Master Brevax that two members of The Thirteen may be involved, hinting at the possibility of another Kanarzand-like situation emerging.

Master Brevax furrows his brow. "That's a political matter far beyond my station. If it's true, it will come to light eventually. I'm just an old professor. I'll keep a watchful eye, but I'm not choosing sides. My job is to report what I've observed, and you can trust me to be discreet about the artefact. It's clearly not of Aystar origin; it's a shard I've never seen before. I'll leave the mystery intact, so if anyone interrogates me, they won't get the full truth."

Aidan nods in understanding, choosing to say nothing more.

Under cover of darkness, aided by concealment spells, the expedition members dispersed, moving through the city to an Old Quarter safe-house. After debriefing and being sworn to secrecy, Ahlissa's crew assisted with delivering the Aethyr Shard to the Aystaran Embassy.

As they moved through the dark streets and alleyways, Aidan pulled Jillian aside to discuss the language the Baron spoke. "He said, 'There is one who will claim you, and your time is short. He already knows you.'" Aidan realised that the language the Baron used was identical in tone and dialect to what he overheard Mhorvaeus speaking during Ahlissa's recent supply mission to Sindarr. The language of the dead; rare and deeply sinister.

Jillian, intrigued, asked, "Who would claim you? Who knows you?"

"There's only one person who fits," Aidan responded. "At a trade negotiation with Ahlissa, I overheard Mhorvaeus speaking the same language."

Aidan recalled that, during their visit to Mhorvaeus' residence, they had speculated that he might be connected to the Servants of Aroth, a dangerous sect devoted to resurrecting the original vampire. Lord Khannay, Aidan's former benefactor from his training in Gideon City, and later his patron to Kanarzand's library, was also suspected of being involved. Now, with the Baron, it seemed another piece of the puzzle was falling into place.

Aidan shared this with Jillian. "Mhorvaeus, Lord Khannay, and now the Baron; all seemed linked to this same sinister cause."

Jillian looked concerned. "And the soldiers of the Jade Talon? Where did they fit in? Were these groups working together? Were they both seeking the item we'd claimed?"

Aidan shrugged. "I had a feeling this item was ancient; going back to the time when the Kale Ashtari left. Maybe they seeded a dynasty of some kind, and I could be connected to it. This artefact was likely a key to unlocking important knowledge."

"Perhaps dark knowledge," Jillian suggested. "We needed to study it carefully, in case it revealed something dangerous."

Aidan nodded. "Some of the languages inscribed on it were dark, but others were not. I wondered if all these dialects once shared a common origin."

"Or possibly even the language of my people," Jillian mused. "Though that would be surprising, given that we came from the far reaches of the Eternal Void."

"Maybe it depended on when this artefact was created and who was around at the time. Plus, we'd never encountered an Aethyr Shard of this size or type. Perhaps it fell from the sky, rather than being unearthed."

"Yet there we were, deep underground," Jillian said thoughtfully. "The Undercity might have been the surface once, but ages of conflict and geological shifts buried it."

"And layer upon layer of cities have been built over it since."

"Guard your discovery well," Jillian advised. "I hoped it revealed everything you were seeking."

25

Deciphering the Stone

Upon arriving at the Aystaran Embassy, Aidan and the others were greeted by Ambassador Aren Shivaleth, who led them deep into the tower's secure chambers. "These rooms are shielded from prying eyes and spells," he assured them. "Your discovery is significant, and if word got out, it would surely attract attention. Rest assured, it will remain protected within these walls. Was the item difficult to obtain?"

One of Ahlissa's senior crew members spoke in Aystaran, summarizing the expedition. He recounted the tense encounter with the self-proclaimed Queen of the Undercity and the battle with soldiers of the Jade Talon. Their force had been led by a priest of the Dark Religion and a noble from Sindarr, who displayed disturbing, possibly undead qualities. All were vanquished, the crew member explained.

Aidan stepped forward to add his thoughts. "I spoke with Master Brevax. He wouldn't report our suspicions about the true nature of the Baron. He's also determined that the item we recovered is a new type of Aethyr Shard, but he won't share that detail either. What we have here is an extraordinary artefact, and it's waiting for us to unlock its secrets."

The ambassador listened thoughtfully, then nodded. "That is wise. Master Brevax has earned our trust. He's worked with us on Aystaran artifacts before, and we've helped him fill in gaps in his knowledge of our history. This artefact you've recovered shows signs of immense power. You are welcome to stay within the embassy compound to conduct your research. Your companion is also welcome. We have always welcomed Khystar to our fold. If Jillian wishes, we can provide her with a new identity and resettlement to Kharadia to ensure her safety."

Jillian, visibly relieved, nodded. "I am very grateful for your offer. A new identity would help me distance myself from the Aldrosian Zealots who may still be searching for me. However, I'm also curious about the artefact," she said, looking at Aidan. "Would you like me to stay? I may not be a scholar, but I'd be happy to assist."

Aidan, pleased by her offer, responded eagerly. "Yes, I'd love for you to stay. It would be great to have you around."

"Then it's settled," Jillian said with a smile. "I'll accept a new identity and help you study the artefact. It sounds like an exciting challenge, and for the first time in months, I feel safe here."

The ambassador smiled warmly. "Excellent. My servants will show you to your private quarters. When you're ready to begin your studies, simply call, and they'll escort you to the chamber where the artefact is securely stored. You are safe here. The embassy is sovereign territory, and no external forces will breach these walls, regardless of whatever grievances may exist between nations."

Aidan and Jillian were shown to their private quarters, while Ahlissa's crew celebrated their successful expedition in the guest quarters. Before the crew departed, Aidan wrote a note for Ahlissa, detailing his brief conversation with Baron Von-Claagen during the encounter, which he entrusted to a crew member to deliver upon their return.

Later, in the quiet of their shared facility, Jillian and Aidan found themselves alone. The atmosphere was calm, a stark contrast to the tension of the underground expedition.

"You performed well in that dangerous mission," Jillian mused. "You didn't seem afraid at all. Perhaps it's the Kale Khestari blood in you. So, when do you plan to start your research on the artefact?"

"Tomorrow," Aidan replied.

Jillian nodded. "I'm looking forward to seeing what we'll discover."

The following morning, Aidan, Jillian, and a team of Aystaran scholars gathered to begin their work. The artefact - an Aethyr Shard of unusual size and energy - stood in the centre of the room, surrounded by protective wards.

Over the next five months, Aidan delved deep into the research. During this time, his once-frequent nightmares subsided, yet his obsession with the artefact grew stronger with each passing day. He felt a powerful pull toward the Aethyr Shard, a strange magnetism that both fascinated and unnerved him.

From the start, it was clear that the Aethyr Shard was protected by numerous magical defences. Aidan's knowledge of spell craft allowed him to detect the first of many layers: a powerful warding spell, which he successfully dispelled. As he continued, he discovered a misdirection effect – permanent and immune to dispelling – that prevented any form of divination. The Aystar priests assisted, using their abilities to try to divine the artefact's origins.

Skill challenges arose. First, the wards and arcane lock barriers were removed, but soon after, a protective effect targeted the scholars, rendering them unconscious for several hours. Aidan avoided its effects and waited patiently for them to recover. Next, a dark ray of energy struck Aidan, draining his strength and causing him to collapse. As darkness overtook him, he heard Jillian's frantic shouts.

When Aidan awakened, he was in a healing chamber, bathed in soft light and serene music. An Aystar healer approached. "How are you feeling?" she asked.

"Weak, but better," Aidan replied. "The artefact drained my strength when I touched it."

Jillian hovered nearby, visibly concerned.

The healer handed Aidan a small blue crystal. "Hold this," she said.

Aidan took it, and as he did, a wave of energy coursed through him, restoring his strength. "Are you ready to continue your study of the artefact?" she asked. "You've been unconscious for three days. We were all worried."

"Yes, I feel much better now," Aidan replied. "Let's continue."

Returning to the chamber, Aidan learned from the scholars that the artefact had not caused any further harm since the incident. His investigation continued, revealing layer upon layer of intricate knowledge stored within the Aethyr Shard.

Each layer contained a new puzzle; languages to be deciphered, symbols to be interpreted. Aidan found himself drawn to a particular section where Aystaran script glowed faintly. As he reached out to touch it, the Aethyr Shard pulsed with a brief orange glow. It felt almost alive, and each time he interacted with it, he felt an unsettling sensation; a crawling under his skin. The taint within him, dormant for months, flared up again, making him feel constantly uncomfortable.

Aidan struggled to resist the pull of the shard, knowing that something malevolent lay within. His attunement to darker knowledge helped him decode three or four layers over the course of a week, but it also revealed troubling insights. The shard's inscriptions suggested it could be a vessel; perhaps a container for something powerful, yet undefined.

As the weeks stretched into months, Aidan decoded ten layers. The languages were a chaotic mix; Aystar, Argar, Khestar, Khystar, and others he couldn't identify. One fragment, written in an obscure dialect, suggested a location in the Forbidden Wastes that might hold further secrets. However, the name of the location remained unclear.

Jillian, noticing Aidan's growing obsession, encouraged him to take breaks from the research. "You're becoming consumed by this," she warned gently. "You need to step away sometimes."

Aidan agreed, though reluctantly. "You're right," he said. "I'll take a break, but we'll just walk in the embassy gardens. The Observers might still be watching outside."

The two spent time walking in the gardens, enjoying the sun and fresh air. They laughed and talked, a brief respite from the intense research. Jillian told Aidan that Ahlissa was worried about him as well. "She thinks the shard is taking hold of you."

"It doesn't control me," Aidan insisted. "I can step away when I need to. I know there's more to life than this artefact." He promised to write to Ahlissa once a week, to keep her updated on his thoughts and progress.

As they returned to the research chamber, Aidan felt renewed determination but also a cautious awareness of the artefact's power.

As another month of study passed, Aidan deciphered a new layer of runes within the Aethyr Shard, revealing secrets about the ancient Kale Ashtari civilization. According to the text, the Kale Ashtari were settlers from the Eternal Void who built the fabled city of Qualtesh, only for it to be destroyed and submerged beneath Scylla's surface during a cataclysmic storm. Forced to survive in these ruined depths, the Kale Ashtari harnessed dark, subterranean energies to combat the shadow creatures and flying demons they encountered in this perilous underworld. Some Kale Ashtari ultimately returned to the surface, while others remained below, adapting to the treacherous conditions beneath the ground. Aidan began to suspect that the ancient Star Haunt ruins he discovered were once inhabited by these Kale Ashtari survivors.

Excited by the prospect of unlocking further secrets, Aidan shared his findings with the Aystaran scholars, drawing connections between the Kale Ashtari's survival strategies and the Shard's own properties. He theorized that, like the Kale Ashtari, the Aethyr Shard embodied a morally ambiguous power. Though it contained dark energies, the Shard might not be intrinsically evil, but rather a vessel transformed by necessity and circumstance, much like the Kale Ashtari themselves.

Following these revelations, Aidan began experiencing vivid, recurring dreams. In his visions, he stood on the prow of an airship amidst a furious storm, navigating a barren, unyielding landscape. The scene evoked a deep sense of belonging, as if the destination and path ahead were tied to his destiny. Each time, his dream ended with the feeling of a hand grasping his shoulder just as he turned to see who it was, and he awakened before finding out.

As he continued his studies, Aidan discovered that he must unlock yet another layer within the Shard. His attempt to dispel the artefact's wards, however, failed spectacularly, unleashing a burst of bright orange light. An inexplicable force compelled Aidan to journey to the Forbidden Wastes, though he did not know why. All he felt was an intense, magnetic pull from the Shard that pointed Northeast, its glowing core illuminating the direction.

Aidan informed the scholars and his allies that the Shard "wanted" to go to the Forbidden Wastes. This declaration alarmed the scholars, who feared the inherent dangers such a journey posed. A messenger was quickly dispatched to the Aystaran Ambassador, Aren Shivaleth, who arrived shortly after to hear Aidan's account. The Ambassador, realising the artefact's urgency, agreed that the Aethyr Shard must be transported, albeit with utmost care, as it would undoubtedly attract attention.

Ahlissa was summoned to consult on the journey. She proposed fortifying the Zephyr Breeze's central storage compartments with both physical and magical protections to secure the Shard and render it undetectable. Ahlissa estimated that these modifications would take two days to complete, giving Aidan time to prepare for the journey.

While discussing the risks, Aidan voiced his hesitation about placing his allies in danger, knowing the threats that the Forbidden Wastes harboured. He suggested enlisting Kale Khestari warriors adept in outdoor survival to provide additional protection. Ahlissa readily agreed, arranging for reinforcements from one of her captain's sister ships. The crew planned to accommodate up to fifty skilled warriors.

Aidan pondered the Shard's moral nature, speculating that it, like the Kale Ashtari, might have absorbed dark power out of necessity rather than an inherent evil. "This intelligence within the Shard," Aidan mused, "could have easily harmed us if it wished. It might contain something malevolent, but if so, it has chosen to reveal its secrets to us rather than act against us." His observations reinforced the Shard's ambiguity and its potential connection to ancient histories and primal forces.

The Ambassador, intrigued, blessed the expedition and offered prayers for a successful journey. "This could be our chance to uncover secrets lost to time, perhaps even to understand the legacy of the Kale Ashtari, a race unknown to our libraries."

Once the preparations were underway, Ahlissa assembled a diverse team for the journey. Besides her crew and the Kale Khestari mercenaries, a small group of Aystaran scholars joined to assist Aidan in deciphering the Shard's layered texts. Jillian was invited to come along as well, and Aidan personally asked her to join. Eager to distance herself from the Aldrosian Zealots who once pursued her, she accepted, embracing the opportunity to explore new places; even the Forbidden Wastes.

In private, Ahlissa assured Aidan that only her crew and the Aystaran Ambassador were aware of the Shard's presence on board. She had informed her superiors at the Glass Tower about the mission, explaining it as a routine training exercise and commercial endeavour to deflect inquiries from groups such as the Seeker or other Council members. This cover story was also designed to mislead the other sinister groups and academic institutions that had shown an interest in the Zephyr Breeze and Ahlissa's activities; the Silent Crescent, the Jade Talon, the Sceptre Guilds, the Observers, the Mhargrave Outreach Society and potentially the Servants of Aroth. All of them represented a clear and present danger.

With fifty Kale Khestari warriors on board, the Zephyr Breeze was ready to depart. Joining the team was a mysterious figure, cloaked and cowled, representing the enigmatic Kale Ereshkigal. A Deathless One. Ahlissa spoke of this figure in reverent tones, hinting at his significance as an observer of the journey's outcome.

Ahlissa approached Aidan as he reviewed the maps sprawled across the table in the ship's planning room. She crossed her arms, watching him for a moment before speaking.

"Aidan, there's something I thought you'd want to know," she said, drawing his attention. "Mistress Sainar reached out. She's provided additional support for our mission; a team from the New Kanarzand Bureau of Forbidden Archaeology."

Aidan raised an eyebrow, looking both intrigued and wary. "The Bureau of Forbidden Archaeology?" he echoed. "That's... quite a specialised group; I am grateful they helped us escape from the Undercity."

Ahlissa smiled knowingly. "You'd be surprised at how much they already know about the Aethyr Shard. Mistress Sainar thought their expertise might prove invaluable, especially in dealing with such an artefact."

"Have they... had any contact with the Shard before?" Aidan asked, his voice tinged with curiosity.

"Not directly," Ahlissa replied, "but they've researched similar relics tied to ancient civilizations and their connections to dark magic. They'll join us once we reach Cordovar."

Aidan nodded thoughtfully. "If Mistress Sainar trusts them, then they might be just what we need."

Ahlissa smiled. "Glad you agree. They'll bring fresh insights and... well, a bit of intrigue, if nothing else."

As the Zephyr Breeze departed from Gideon City, Aidan stood at the ship's railing, gazing out over the distant cityscape fading behind them. The enormity of the mission ahead settled heavily on him, and he hadn't realised he was frowning until he felt Jillian approach. She stepped up beside him, quiet, then placed a gentle hand on his arm.

"Lost in thought already?" she asked softly, glancing up at him. Aidan exhaled, nodding.

"Just... thinking," he replied, his voice carrying a hint of doubt. He turned toward her, worry in his gaze. "Am I doing the right thing, Jillian? I feel like I'm doing this for the right reasons, but... it's hard to shake the feeling that this is somehow outside my control."

She looked at him thoughtfully, weighing her words. "Perhaps," she said slowly, "you are following the right path, but I am worried that something else is guiding you." She gestured gently toward the faint glow of the Aethyr Shard, secured within the ship's storage but still faintly visible from where they stood. "There's an undeniable pull to it, Aidan. Do you feel it too?"

He nodded, unable to deny the sensation. "Every time I get closer to understanding the Shard, it feels like something inside me responds. Like a... voice, or a tether that's drawing me in."

"Have you ever thought," she ventured, meeting his eyes with gentle concern, "that maybe that pull isn't entirely yours? That perhaps the Shard has its own purpose, and it might not be one we fully understand?"

Aidan hesitated, glancing back toward the secure storage below decks. He felt the weight of her words. "I have thought about it. But... what if it's my only chance to understand where I came from, my connection to these lost people, the Kale Ashtari?"

"That's a powerful reason," she acknowledged. "But remember, it's possible to be driven too far by what's within us. And... you could lose something of yourself along the way."

Aidan looked away, absorbing her words. "So... you think I might be sacrificing myself for something that isn't really mine?"

"Not exactly. I think you might be walking the line. There's no denying the Shard's connection to you, or to the knowledge you're seeking. But I worry that connection may also come with a price." She paused, watching him. "That's why I agreed to come on this journey, to help you hold onto yourself."

He managed a faint smile at her words. "You keep me grounded. Remind me that I'm not doing this alone. Sometimes I forget."

She chuckled softly. "And you don't need to carry the weight alone, Aidan. We're all in this with you. If the Shard has a hold on you, then I'll help you keep it at bay. Just promise me you'll keep one eye on the path; and the other on yourself."

Aidan placed his hand over hers, feeling a renewed sense of strength. "I promise. And if I start to lose my way... you'll be there to remind me who I am."

26

A Dark Calling

One night, as the crew slept and the ship sped silently through the darkness, Aidan woke suddenly.

The pull of the Shard was stronger than ever, an insistent force that demanded his attention. He rose from his bed and made his way to the secure storage, his heart pounding with a mixture of fear and anticipation.

The Shard lay on a pedestal, its crystalline surface glowing with an otherworldly light. Aidan approached it slowly, his breath coming in shallow gasps. He reached out a trembling hand, his fingers brushing against the cool, smooth surface of the stone.

In an instant, a surge of energy coursed through him, a powerful wave that left him gasping for breath. He felt the presence of the Shard, a dark, malevolent force that seemed to wrap itself around his very soul.

"*Aidan,*" the voice whispered in his mind, a sinister echo that sent shivers down his spine. "*You are mine.*"

He tried to pull away, but the Shard's grip was too strong. He felt himself being drawn deeper into its embrace, his will bending to its power. Images flashed before his eyes, visions of destruction and chaos, of a world consumed by darkness.

"No," he whispered, his voice barely audible. "I won't let you control me."

The voice laughed, a cold, mocking sound. *"You have no choice. You sought the truth, and now you are bound to it. Embrace the darkness, Aidan. Let it consume you."*

Summoning every ounce of willpower, Aidan forced his hand away from the Shard. The effort left him trembling, beads of sweat forming on his brow. He staggered back, his mind reeling from the encounter. He knew now, more than ever, that the Shard was not merely an object of power but a sentient force with its own dark agenda.

And he knew it had him in its thrall.

Glossary

Adeni

Equivalent to humans in common fantasy settings; mostly civilised and users of magic and technology. Some nomadic tribal groups do exist. The Adeni do accept the Argar as workers in cities and towns and engage with the Aystar for politics, trade and academic research.

Age of Calamity

This was the Fourth Age. It was a period of time in which all the nations waged bitter warfare against each other. It is also the time when vast natural disasters occurred, including the devastation wrought by a great celestial body from the Eternal Void that led to the fall of the Aystar Kingdom, the destruction of the Argar Empire, the demise of Hapt-Sept Amun's city, and the formation of the Tahnaar Desert and its wider region on the continent of Syrnadar.

Age of Creation

This was the Third Age when the Khestar transitioned to become the Aystar factions of the Kale Khestari and Kale Ashtari.This is also the time when the Aethyric realm of Aldrosia remained to conceal the continued existence of the Khystar in a separate state of reality.

Age of Darkness

This was the First Age when the world of Scylla formed but was dominated and consumed by dark shadowy entities and evil creatures. Aroth, the First Vampire, rose to prominence at this time.

Age of Dreams

This was the Second Age, and it is the period of time when the Khestar and Khystar people arrived from the Eternal Void in their ethereal form and settled in the continent of Kharadia, ultimately harnessing the light strands of Aethyr to manifest and build the physical world.

Age of Rediscovery

This is the Fifth Age. It is the current period of time in which the Adeni, Aystar and Argar people are tolerant yet mistrustful of one another. The world of Scylla is dominated by many factions and power groups as a result and espionage is commonplace.

Aethyr

This is the primordial, mystical force or energy that provides magic to the world. It exists in positive or negative influence, commonly referenced as light or dark, and manifests in sentient beings as good or evil. The essence of Aethyr can be condensed and stored in crystals and stones, which are used to augment magical spells, imbue special powers into items or activate arcane energy devices.

Ahlissa

The independent captain and resourceful owner of the airship The Zephyr Breeze. A smuggler and opportunist with connections to the Argar, she is poised to become an important player, possibly aiding Aidan in his quest with access to rare resources and information.

Aidan

The main protagonist of the story; a half-Aystar scholar and student of magic. In Kharadia, he gains knowledge from the Keepers of the Past and is trained as an Adept in the Temple of the Ages. In order to prove himself an equal, and to be accepted rather than shunned as an outsider, he also trains in the ways of the Kale Khestari as a warrior.

Airships

There are four significant airships operated by the Aystar across the continents of Kharadia and Syrnadar; the Zephyr Breeze, the Zephyr Cloud, the Zephyr Spirit and the Zephyr Storm. Each is powered by a combination of Aethyr and ancient Khestar technology making them very advanced. Other smaller airships and flying vessels exist, operated by the various organisations, political factions and trade guilds of Scylla.

Aldrosia

A mountain sanctuary for the Khystar people seeking to escape the influence of the Zealots of the Dreamlands.

Alira

Captain of the Zephyr Spirit; a skilled tactician, calm and calculating in times of tension.

Althas

Captain of the Guard for Lord Mhorvaeus.

Aren Shivaleth

The Ambassador for the Aystaran people, and liaison for their various factions, usually resident at the Aystaran Embassy in Gideon City.

Argar

Equivalent to orcs in common fantasy settings; mostly subservient to Adeni in civilised areas but proud, self-determining and indignant towards all races in their traditional wilderness enclaves. They identify as high-caste, mid-caste or low-caste groupings based on size (large, medium or small) but some variations of these people are of a monstrous nature, ostracised to the fringes and dark places of the world, even by the Argar.

Aroth

Aroth was the First Vampire in Scylla and her influence was based in the nation of Sindarr. Her followers, the Servants of Aroth, believe she will rise again to reclaim her throne.

Aspiring Dream

The planned purge of Khystar people by Zealots from the Dreamlands.

Aystar

Equivalent to Elven people in common fantasy settings; fair haired, golden eyed, with fast reactions and slender build. Masters of magic and operators of the airships. Tolerant of Adeni people and usually dismissive towards Argar. Mostly distant, aloof and isolationist.

Bakr

The charismatic Agar shaman who leads the So-Kech on their pilgrimage to find El-Mishra on the promises of uncovering their history to reclaim their ancestral homeland.

Baron Von-Claagen

An influential minor noble from Sindarr, leader of a contingent of Jade Talon soldiers and an associate of Lord Khannay; his outward mannerisms and pale complexion caused Aidan and his companions to suspect he was a vampire with possible connections to the Servants of Aroth.

Blue

A sentient dark blue leather-bound book that once channelled the mind and power of Velis, a powerful wizard. Blue connected with Aidan through recognition of his half-Aystar bloodline and gifts him with the ability to tap into greater magic. It no longer communicates with him, its pages now blank. Despite this, Aidan keeps it, clinging to the faint hope that the spirit of the wizard Velis, possibly an ancestor, who was freed from imprisonment but slain in Kanarzand, might one day speak to him again.

Broken Blade Inn

This is where Aidan first encounters The Observers. It is a location that attracts danger and an unwelcoming crowd, on the fringes of New Kanarzand at the edge of Gideon City.

Dark Religion

An overarching cult of evil followers.

Deathless Ones

Revered ancestors who died but were resurrected and persist as undead advisors.

Destari

Followers of The Wasteland Druid. Nomadic, solitary and mostly incorporeal. They have become one with nature and have merged with the elements of sand and wind.

Drazakh Khan

A monstrous Argar warlord who, during the Age of Calamity, uncovered the Dark Aethyr Shard in the Forbidden Wastes and retained it as a great symbol of his power.

El-Mishra

Once a great town, the Capital of the ancient Algarian Empire. Also known as the "Town of the Fallen Star" and said to harbour an ancient power named "The Heart of the Sands".

Eternal Void

This is space and the wider universe in which Scylla is only one world, circling its star, Kyrathia.

Everhold

The largest nomadic Adeni settlement in the Kalos Plains.

Fallen Aystar

This is a term used to identify Aystaran people who follow the Dark Religion. They develop physical Traits, such as pale skin and dark eyes, that reveal they have chosen to follow evil.

Forbidden Wastes

This is a desolate and dangerous location in Syrnadar. It is said to be influenced by monstrous and supernatural entities from the Age of Darkness.

Gideon City

The regional Capital: a Gothic Victorian-styled city ruled by a Magocracy (The Thirteen). It is dominated by magical colleges, industry and trading guilds. Highly political and authoritarian. Policed by a guard force, overseen by The Sentinel.

Hapt-Sept Amun

A maniacal narcissistic self-made God-King, who sought immortality and summoned the power of Aethyr which cursed him and transformed him an unliving being, together with his people. Having been released from his buried city and tomb, he yearns to restore his lost humanity.

Harvin

Captain of the Zephyr Cloud airship; a seasoned Adeni known for his sharp eye and unmatched instincts in evasive manoeuvres.

High King Iaeras I

The ruler of the Kale Khestari war clans.

House of Tyrelis

Ahlissa referenced this group as being able to assist Aidan with his deviant Aethyr Mark; but at the cost of being exploited by them for the power it may give.

Ivistar Immiar

Ahlissa is betrothed to Ivistar Immiar, a hot-headed Warlord of the Kale Khestari and a favoured warrior of High King Iaeras I. He frequently stirs conflict along the Aystaran borders, seeking to prove the honour of the Kale Khestari. Admiring Ahlissa's bold actions in Kanarzand, he tolerates Aidan but sees him as weak, often reminding him of this despite Ahlissa's scolding, which he ignores.

Izen'draazt

The Ageless One. The Dark Destroyer. The Endless Night. This ancient evil demon from the Eternal Void brings chaos to every world that it touches, bringing with it corruption and destruction. The creatures that its power touches become transformed into horrid fearsome things, colloquially known as "Unforgiven", and impervious to all ordinary weapons. There is a rare dark-red crystalline mineral present in the Tahnaar Desert that, when infused with light Aethyr and treated with the Tears of Diamh, can forge weapons that harm Izen'draazt's minions or hold them at bay.

Jillian

One of the Khystar people, a shapeshifter and the last of her kind in Syrnadar.

Kaldorin

This is the location of a small town and military staging post, built on the ruins of a ruined citadel.

Kale Ashtari

A dark natured bloodline of Khestar; Aidan fears his ancestry is linked to them.

Kale Ereshkigal

Known as the Deathless Ones, or revered ancestors, of the Aystar. They are said to be a generation removed from the Khestar and have been present for centuries. They are undead but are not malevolent or hostile towards living creatures.

Kale Khestari

Descended from the Khestar, these nomadic Aystaran people, a proud and intolerant warrior-caste acclimatised to long desert patrols and warfare against wild monsters and predators. Their ancestral homeland is centred on Sunhold which is located in Kharadia.

Kale Khaestas

A large desert fortress, home base of the Kale Khestari war clans.

Kanarzand

The gothic wild-western-styled frontier town in the desert, ruled by the Wizards Council (The Twelve) who have pledged allegiance to The Thirteen. Despite the semblance of authority, lawlessness is rife and the explorer/discovery guilds have great influence because they bring the finance. Danger is everywhere and both Adeni and Argar people are drawn here to seek fortune and adventure as mercenaries in the surrounding sands and ruins.

Keeper of the Past

A title provided to respected elders in the Temple of the Ages.

Kharadia

One of the continents that exist in the world of Scylla. It is the continent where the Aystar and Khystar people originate from.

Khestar

This was the ancient progenitor race, forefathers to the Aystar, who travelled the Eternal Void in vessels powered by Aethyr. They brought their magic and items of wondrous power to continents of Kyrathia and Syrnadar when their culture spanned the globe in an Age of Enlightenment.

Kyrathia

This is the name of the star around which the planet Scylla orbits, in the Eternal Void.

Kyshtar

An ancient race that co-inhabited the world alongside the Aystar after arriving from the Eternal Void independently. Known as shapeshifters, the Adeni wizards sought to eliminate them, believing that "their kind" are dangerous for being aberrations to natural order.

Lake Glassmere

Located near the border where the Tahnaar Desert ends and the Kalos Plains begin.

Liberty Spire

This is a place frequented by the elite and wealthy of Gideon City. Ahlissa takes Aidan here one evening, after concluding his adventures with the Kale Khestari in Kharadia.

Lorian Tyraleth

A stern and accomplished war band leader. He is Aidan's martial lore tutor.

Lord Khannay

Lord Khannay was the benefactor of the library in Kanarzand and Aidan's patron. He was rumoured to be a vampire and aligned with the Servants of Aroth and Baron Von-Claagen.

Magocracy

A ruling council of wizards and magicians; in Gideon City this is The Thirteen and in Kanarzand this is The Twelve.

Master Brevax

Aidan's mentor. An elderly historian in Gideon City.

Mhargrave Outreach Society

One of the greedy archaeological factions that dominates and influences political and academic activity across all Kharadia and Syrnadar. Aidan briefly disrupts their activity when he encounters the Rogue Mercenaries at one of their dig sites in the Tahnaar Desert.

Mistress Sainar

The pragmatic and cunning Guild mistress of the Kanarzand Bureau of Forbidden Archaeology. She's an influential figure concerned about profit, knowledge control, and maintaining balance in the city. Her increasing interest in Aidan's activities marks her as a potential threat or reluctant ally.

Monks at the Temple of Twilight Calm

Ahlissa has told Aidan that this religious order may be able to help him remove the Aethyr Mark. He does not know much about them, except they offer healing in exchange for services or donations.

Oren

Oren is one of Aidan's initial companions, a former Sentinel guard from Gideon City, who leads Aidan to follow Bakr and the So-Kech to find El-Mishra. He proves himself invaluable with his quick thinking and tactical skills. His goal is to protect the desert's people from the growing darkness, fighting both external threats and the treachery of rival factions.

Ostarr

A large town at the border of Sindarr. The Citadel of Mhorvaeus is located in the hills nearby.

Queen Ashkaan

Queen Ashkaan, the iron-fisted ruler of the Argar quarter in Gideon's Old Undercity, is a towering figure of menace and mystery. Ashkaan's most defining feature is the intricately crafted metal helmet she wears at all times, a dark, spiked visage that covers her face and eyes completely. The helmet's sinister design, forged with jagged patterns and moulded to fit her head seamlessly, gives her a nightmarish, almost otherworldly appearance. It is said that the metal she chose is rare, imbued with an ancient enchantment, which she claims prevents any magic from removing it or seeing through it. Her followers believe this helmet is not merely for intimidation; Ashkaan's helmet conceals something much more terrifying beneath.

Rogue Mercenaries

An Argar farmer with a lost heritage of great prestige, a mechanical creation imbued with a living soul, a low-caste Adeni priest, and a former dishonourably discharged Sentinel guard from Gideon City; this group had been gaining quite an unfortunate reputation in Kanarzand recently with their exploits and after hearing of Aidan uncovering forbidden magic (and encountering him at a Mhargrave Dig Site) they have vowed to hunt him down for bounty, on behalf of The Twelve.

Sceptre Guilds

Twelve primary houses that are aligned to particular Aethyr Marks, which in turn associate them directly with specific functions, such as trade, espionage, etc.

Scornland

A dangerous place; destroyed by horrific magic during the Age of Calamity. The land itself is cursed. Any survivors of that cataclysm have been twisted into monsters. Healing magic doesn't work there, and the entire area is prone to violent magical storms.

Scylla

The name of the world setting for the fantasy novel; synonymous with danger.

Servants of Aroth

A fanatical cult devoted to the worship of Aroth, the First Vampire in Scylla.

Shaevath Tyrathalas

A venerable elder Keeper of the Past, and Aidan's mentor at the Temple of the Ages in Kharadia.

Silent Crescent

One of the most aggressive, clandestine and fanatical archaeological research factions; they seek ancient Khestar artefacts and are well known to Captain Ahlissa as serious competitors to her operations.

Sindarr

This is a warlike nation that aligns itself with the Dark Religion and promotes necromancy.

So-Kech

A significant religious grouping of Argar, led by a powerful Shaman named Bakr. Collectively regarded as a cult, they are also known as "Word Bearers".

Spark Rail

A train that connects Kanarzand and Gideon City across the vast expanse of the Tahnaar desert. It is magically powered and glides overland, emitting lightning around it, hence its name.

Star Haunt

This ancient, ruined place was a fortress for the Kale Ashtari, the dark bloodline of the ancient Khestar. This is where Aidan discovers his first clues and suspects his heritage may be linked to them, after his encounter with the tainted guardian.

Sunhold

The spiritual centre of knowledge and High Capital city of the Aystar people on the continent of Kharadia.

Syrnadar

One of the continents that exist in the world of Scylla. It is where the primary story locations of Gideon City and Kanarzand are located, in the middle of the Tahnaar Desert.

Tahnaar Desert

An ancient Adeni name, it was given when the three ancient empires existed.

Taint

A condition that relates to an unnatural or dark influence by something, possibly a form of possession by another entity or corruption by exposure to Dark Aethyr.

Temple of the Ages

A bastion of knowledge, its grand halls are filled with the histories and legends of the Khestar, the progenitors of the Aystaran people.

Terror Lizards

Giant carnivorous reptiles that roam the Kalos Plains.

Thalendir

An ancient king of the High-Aystaran people, a direct descendant of the Khestar and Kale Khestari. His remains have a special meaning to the scattered Aystaran people.

The Glass Tower

A covert network that operates across Scylla, primarily connecting half-Aystar operatives. Their goal isn't to control Scylla, but to keep it balanced. They gather knowledge and intervene when necessary to prevent another devastating conflict like the Age of Calamity.

The Guard Post of Athosin

This is a small stone tower of Athosin, surrounded by a few modest outbuildings, which functions as an outpost for Kale Khestari warriors.

The Jade Talon

A sinister mercenary group comprised predominantly of Argar.

The Machination

An organisation that Ahlissa works for, answerable to a group called The Glass Tower.

The Observers

These three mysterious and enigmatic individuals are working for The Thirteen and are hunting for anyone who displays signs of bearing a deviant Aethyr Mark.

The Prism

This is the name given by The Glass Tower to The Zephyr Breeze, to highlight its importance as an asset to The Machination.

The Rogue Mercenaries

An unusual group causing unrest in the desert, including a dishon-ourably discharged Sentinel guard, a mechanical creation with a soul, an Argar tribesman, and a low-caste Adeni priest. They've inadvertently triggered chaos by slaughtering a nest of Zar'tul and aligning with the Mhargrave Outreach Society. After the fall of Kanarzand, the merce-naries eventually confronted Izen'draazt and defeated the monstrous entity.

The Shard of Drazakh Khan

A large dark Aethyr Shard that is protected by strange magic and requires research to unlock its secrets. Aidan believes it holds the key to answering many mysteries about the origins of Scylla.

The Thirteen

The rulers of Gideon City; The Seeker, The Gatherer, The Hunter, The Sentinel, The Maker, The Communicator, the Traveller and six others. Also known as the High Magocracy.

The Twelve

The paranoid and xenophobic rulers of Kanarzand; led by Saius, an ambitious and cruel wizard who desires control and power to rival that of The Thirteen. They wish to suppress all knowledge of anything that might challenge their claim to authority. Also known as the Arcane Council.

Tiralas

A young warrior of the Kale Khestari who befriends Aidan and is a valued friend.

Velis

An ancient half-Aystar wizard that uncovered forbidden magic, resulting in his exile and imprisonment. Through Blue, he communicates with Aidan.

Vyrethen

An Aystar advisor from the homeland in Kyrathia. Knowledgeable about the ancient Khestar.

Wasteland Druid

An ancient cursed Adeni man whose fate is tied to the Tahnaar Desert region. He masters the power of Aethyr to control the environment, bending it to his will and shaping the land. His followers are known as the Desari, or Dust Whisperers, and his power is a rival to Izen'draazt.

Wayne Scarrow

Wayne is a "Fixer" and initially presents himself as a kind benefactor on Aidan's arrival in Kanarzand. He is a manipulator who has positioned himself as a broker of information and a shrewd dealmaker, prone to outbursts of jealousy if he does not get things going his way.

Zar'tul

The sinister, demon-worshiping desert snake people who were discovered by both the academic and mercenary groups. Their extermination has upset the fragile balance with the Argar and hinted at darker forces lurking beneath the sands. There are two types of these creatures; warrior caste and shape shifters.

Zealots of Aldrosia

A generic term used to describe the fanatical Aldrosians who subscribe to the Aspiring Dream and seek to hunt down Aldrosian separatists across Scylla.

Zenot

One of the priests that accompanied the expedition to retrieve the Dark Aethyr Shard from the Undercity.

Zephyr Breeze

Captain Ahlissa's pride and joy. It operates with a mixed Adeni and Argar crew. This is one of four known Aystar magically powered vessels which also incorporate ancient Khestar technology.

Zephyr Cloud

Slightly smaller and faster than the Zephyr Breeze, this airship is often used as a scout or messenger.

Zephyr Spirit

This is a formidable airship, carrying heavier weaponry than its counterparts.

Zephyr Storm

This airship is used to conduct diplomacy, trade and other missions in the Tahnaar Desert region.

Also by Brad Williams

The Kanarzand Trilogy was produced and released between October-December 2024.

Learn more at: https://www.darkenwildepublishing.link/

KANARZAND (Book One)
Aidan, a half-Aystar scholar, becomes the target of powerful factions after awakening ancient magic linked to his heritage.

Hunted by jealous wizards, mercenaries, cultists and other adversaries, Aidan enlists the help of his new allies, including Oren, Captain Ahlissa, and Jillian, an alien shapeshifter.

Together, they embark on a dangerous journey to uncover the truth behind the hidden magic and expose the secrets of the desert.

The Dead King's Bones (Book Two)

Aidan journeys with Ahlissa and Jillian, to Sunhold, in Kharadia, to repatriate the long-lost bones of King Thalendir. In doing so, he is welcomed among the Aystar and learns about his people and their bloodlines, ultimately training as a warrior to be accepted by them.

Aidan faces new trials in the desert while, haunted by visions and terrifying nightmares, he discovers that he bears an abnormal magical mark that is associated with a dark forgotten heritage.

New threats emerge and the companions find themselves in a race against rivals to retrieve an ancient artefact from deep beneath Gideon City.

Demon Stone (Book Three)

Aidan finds himself held in the thrall of a dangerous and malevolent entity as he obsessively researches and deciphers the magic inscriptions that the Dark Aethyr Shard bears.

Aidan, Ahlissa, Jillian and their allies embark on a quest through ruins and labyrinths, uncovering secrets that link Aidan to the lost Kale Ashtari, and which lead them to rediscover the ancient lost city of Qualtesh in the Forbidden Wastes.

Demon Stone is a sweeping tale of ancient legacies, dark magic and the enduring fight for hope and unity in a fractured world.

www.ingramcontent.com/pod-product-compliance
Lightning Source LLC
Chambersburg PA
CBHW060632260626
47161CB00008B/2872